Dear,
This one she
of the old

SANTORINI
(A NOVEL)

SANTORINI
(A NOVEL)

———

Peter W. Katsirubas

ISBN-13: 9781548228484
ISBN-10: 1548228486

Must we go farther and call
no man happy so long as he
is alive? Must we in Solon's
phrase, 'look to the end?'

ARISTOTLE

To be or not to be, that is the question.

SHAKESPEARE

There is but one truly serious philosophical
problem and that is suicide.

ALBERT CAMUS

CONTENTS
August 1973

MONDAY NIGHT

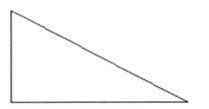

CHAPTER 1

"SOON YOU'LL SEE IT CLEARLY, the Lost Continent of Atlantis," someone said.

Without a moon the sea was black as pitch; a fluid void flowing up against the unseen cliffs of the Greek island of Santorini.

Three launches labored toward the shore. Behind them the deck lights of the ship *Elektra* diminished in size. As they lunged low in the water, a cold salt spray drifted over their passengers. Their gas engines chugged monotonously sputtering puffs of fumes and bursts of cinders that sparkled in and disappeared into the dark.

Standing in the third launch, Stephen could see an assembly of lights on the shore. His eyes strained them in then followed a sparse, zigzag trail of bulbs to the top of the cliff where a larger collection of them shone less potently through a veiling haze. He heard the barrel-chested man at the rudder shout a command and watched his two hands react when the tread-bare tires draped over the vessel's sides struck the cement pier.

The dock was populated with male islanders who had descended the cliff to rent the tourists donkeys and horses for the arduous ascent to the small town of Thira. With a Pan Am flight bag in each hand, Stephen spotted the boy and motioned him over.

"Are you Renas Trekas' son?" he asked him in Greek.

"Yes," said the boy.

"Is he down here now?"

"Up above."

"If you see him before I do tell him the American Stephanos would like to rent one of his rooms. He'll remember me from last summer. I wrote good things about him in that book he shows the tourist."

"Do you have a ride?"

"Not yet."

"All of my animals have tourists but I could come back for you in half an hour."

"I'll be over there," Stephen pointed toward the canvas awning of a small café that flapped to the cadence of the sea breeze.

It was the lights of that café and a smaller one at the opposite end of the dock that illuminated the area. Their lights, like beacons in the off-shore darkness, in proximity were dim and streaked long shadows across the landing. The interplay of silhouettes added to the frenetic atmosphere of new arrivals and their urgency to find rides and accommodations.

Stephen sat at one of the café's low, metal tables and ordered *ouzo* from the proprietor who stood behind a dented freezer on the verandah selling bottled drinks. Through a crowd of babbling tongues, he could see the Trekas boy collecting his customers. Bargains were struck at prices varying with the rider and amount of luggage and personal naiveté.

Two blasts from the *Elektra*'s horn echoed the eerie reverberation of her departure. The ship reduced to a skeleton of lights as the voices of tourists strayed from the dock to behind the café where the animals were roped. Their garbles became interspersed with the clatter of hooves and soon too were absorbed by the haunting flow of wind.

Lethargy replaced the mass confusion. The lights of the other café were extinguished. Stephen paid for a second *ouzo* and shifted his chair to face the dark sea. At the far end of the café two young women in sweaters and jeans drank lemon sodas. Their knapsacks rested heavy on the ground beside them like cumbersome, overturned insects. The proprietor delegated his wife and daughter the task of closing up and relaxed at another round table with the barrel-chested captain of the third launch. Aside from them the dock was deserted.

Stephen ran a hand along one of his bags to make sure his gun was safe then swallowed the remainder of his liquor. He felt warm and content and oblivious to all except the salty wind and the indistinct mumble of conversation from the proprietor's table.

"Excuse me," a voice interrupted the tranquil nothingness that engulfed him, "do you speak English?"

"Yes," he said, looking up into the blue eyes of one of the girls from the other table.

"We were afraid you didn't. Nancy and I, I mean," she enunciated her words with a British accent. "We, I was wondering if you knew anything about this island."

"Some."

"Is there a pension here by the sea where we could rent a room?"

"No. This length of the island is a continuous cliff."

"I thought so but Nancy insists she saw some buildings beyond the other café."

"Just a minute."

Stephen leaned back in his chair and confirmed his observations from the proprietor.

"No place down here," he translated for the girl. "Your friend saw the boatmen's shacks. The beaches are at other ends of the island and one has a hotel."

"How would we get there?"

"Tonight?"

"Straightaway. I want to absorb as much Greek sun as possible before returning home to the rain. I want my tan to last all year," she smiled.

"You wouldn't. Tomorrow you can take a taxi or a bus to it but you'll have to spend tonight up in the town."

"I see. Thank you."

The girl returned to her friend. He watched her explain the situation gesturing in his direction in a he-told-me-so manner.

As he became conscious of the fatigue that infected his body and being, Stephen's thoughts drifted. From dawn in Piraeus where he had observed the waiters with their cool morning faces to where his twelve-hour journey had brought him, the images of his day replayed their effects on him. Shipboard was the hollow-face of an old man wrapped in a blanket in a deck chair absorbing the sun's heat like a reptile, returning to his native Crete to die, who had lectured him on women and love. Late afternoon it had been a bare-foot, young girl whose stoic posture and expressionless lips accompanied a song selected on the ship's jukebox about wine and death. What had made her lips impressionable was the way the words she mouthed meant nothing to her; only the unrestrained inflection of her high nasal voice mattered until the record ended and they broadened into a smile acknowledging the approval of her family for whom she had performed.

A duet of laughter broke the trance.

"Good night Kapetan Charon, good sleep," said the proprietor.

"Hope so," the captain replied, walking out of the lights toward the shacks, "and get some rest yourself."

"I'm closing now," the proprietor called out after him.

His parting words and steps brought him to where Stephen sat.

"The Kapetan is an amusing man," he said. "He has a story for every day of the year."

Stephen nodded complacently.

"Are you finished with your drink? I'm closing."

"Yes, take it. I paid your wife."

"I know," said the proprietor taking up the glass and looking to where the girls sat. "Where are they from?"

"England."

"They thought they could sleep down here?"

"Apparently."

The proprietor shook his head disapprovingly.

"Tourists."

"They bring money."

"Not their kind. They come with sleeping bags because they don't want to spend a few drachmas for a room and live on the beach like animals. You should visit here in the daytime, it becomes an asylum. This afternoon a group of them came down to take a boat to the volcano. Have you been?"

"No."

"It's nothing. Yet they came down here, some eight or ten of them, and sat together. Two with beards like priests ordered one orange drink to share, share mind you, and the rest water. And if they sat for half an hour they ordered twenty glasses of water; as if my wife and I had nothing to do but fetch them water."

"But the English girls are different," said Stephen. "They ordered drinks and asked about renting a room."

"And what did you tell them?"

"That they'd have to stay up in the town."

"And what did she say to that?"

"Thank you very much."

"So what are they waiting for? The resurrection? I want to close. They can sleep all day but I must be up at dawn."

"Patience," Stephen offered a Viceroy from his pack, "they're leaving."

The girls were standing. Each helped the other with her knapsack. One last perusal of the ground to make sure they had all their possessions and they moved out into the wind toward the cement stairs and Rue Marinatos.

"She would sleep with you," said the proprietor through smoke exhaled from his nostrils, when the girl who had approached Stephen gestured him good-bye.

Stephen laughed.

"You sound like an old man I spoke with on the ship today."

"In our lives we must have seen the same things."

"We all see the same things. What matters is the way we comprehend them."

"Perhaps I'm no philosopher. How will they get up the cliff?"

"Walk I suppose."

"Do they know how high it is?"

"Would they walk it if they did?"

"Didn't you tell them? It could take them hours with their packs."

"What else have they got to do? In the long run they probably won't mind. It will give them a memory. People travel to encounter the unexpected. They think it helps them find the meaning of life?"

"How are you getting up there?"

"The Trekas boy is bringing me a horse."

The proprietor laughed.

"So you have already found the meaning of life is that it?" he said.

"That or I don't care to find it," said Stephen.

"Then why do you travel? Why are you here?"

"To kill myself."

"Why?"

"Why not?"

The proprietor laughed.

Chapter 2

The horses belonging to the Trekas boy were tired, emaciated beasts. Their round, filmy eyes mirrored their Sisyphean agony of daily descending and ascending the cliff on Rue Marinatos.

Rue Marinatos is a series of five hundred and eighty-seven steps that rise for half a mile into the center of the town of Thira. The cobblestone street was built in a repetitious Z pattern so the animals could climb a milder incline. It is rumored when Greek villagers are exasperated by the stubbornness of their beasts of burden they threaten them with deportation to Santorini. The superstitious believe that the evilest souls of the damned have been condemned to inhabit those saddled, expiring carcasses.

Beside the boy's two horses, three mules and a donkey fed from a communal trough. Having misinterpreted their master's click of tongue, while he collected riders' fees, they had descended the cliff for their next loads. Nearby, the English girls stared up at the town they could not see.

"It's a distance to the top isn't it?" said the girl Stephen had spoken with to get his attention.

"Yes."

"It would be a strenuous climb even without our packs." She left her friend to stand by Stephen. "We had no idea."

"Not many do."

"We shouldn't have stopped for a drink but we were so thirsty."

Her talking around the issue amused him. At last he volunteered:

"You don't have to walk."

"I beg your pardon."

"You and your friend can ride those mules, unless you want the exercise."

"God no," she smiled. "My name is Jill."

"Stephen."

"Oh, and this is…"

"Nancy. You told me in the café."

"Did I?"

Both girls were attractive without being beautiful. Jill was tan and sensuously built with ample breasts and brown hair cut to her shoulders and lightened almost blond in patches by the sun. Nancy was a couple of inches taller, slim and high-hipped with long auburn hair and a very fair complexion. Objectively, he thought Nancy the prettier of the two except when Jill smiled or moved.

"You're lucky," he said after convincing the Trekas boy to fetch the extra mules and donkey.

"How's that?" asked Jill.

"You're getting free rides. Those animals don't belong to the boy. They strayed down here and you're doing their owner, who's probably in bed, a favor by herding them back up."

"What if their owner isn't asleep but waiting for us, what if he doesn't see things the way you do?" Nancy wanted to know, avoiding eye contact with Stephen.

"That won't be the case."

"I suppose you can guarantee it?" Nancy said with an aloofness bordering on sarcasm.

"I can guarantee that you can do as I suggest or walk."

"Of course we'll ride," said Jill. "Nancy didn't mean to sound rude."

"You needn't apologize for me."

"Then don't be such a child Nancy. Will it be difficult to find a place to sleep so late at night?" Jill asked Stephen.

"I plan on renting a room from the boy's father. If you want I'll ask if he can accommodate you two. But let's get going, I'm tired and hungry and…"

About fifteen hundred years before the birth of Christ the mountain island of Santorini exploded in volcanic fury. The eruption collapsed two-thirds of the island deep below the sea, So deep that when a ship moors between crescent-shaped Santorini proper and the three small islands that face it, it cannot drop anchor into solid earth,

The white-washed buildings of Thira town stretch across the center of Santorini's two-mile cliff, softly drooling over its precipitous edge. It is a cramped settlement of narrow, windless alleys

sometimes shaded by an arch of grapevines, sometimes interrupted by a twisted olive tree. Little thought had been awarded to
civic planning. Neighbor built next to and above neighbor until
the society had honeycombed its maze to the point where space
for its needs had given genesis to a town. At night most of its worn
stone paths are shrouded in dark silence; save the lower ones
whose retaining walls trace the exposed cliff. Thira had no main
streets, only two prominent intersecting alleys that bore the dates
of March 25 and April 21, names imposed by the military junta
that seized control of Greece six years before in 1967.

"I'm beginning to doubt the existence of any town up there,"
said Jill, "and this bouncing horse…"

"Mule."

"Whatever is making me sore."

"You'll see Thira as soon as we rise above the fog," said Stephen.

"What's it like up there?" Nancy called out from behind them.

"Mystical."

"What do you mean?

Chapter 3

Renas Trekas stood below the entrance of the town. He was a
thin man with a leathery face that made him look older than his
middle years. By the dismounting platform atop Rue Marinatos,
he could hear the sounds of laboring animals and human voices
but could not see their source until they had passed through the
blend of mist and darkness as though penetrating a gate of clouds.
Suddenly they were upon him. He helped Jill and Nancy down
from their mules before greeting Stephen with a handshake.

"I guessed it was you from my son."

"Last summer you made me promise to accept a favor from you
and a comfortable bed will be it."

"A room, of course, but you said you'd return in June and it is August. I had a private room for you but you didn't come and tonight I only have one unoccupied. It's been cleaned and if you'll stay there tonight other arrangements can be made tomorrow."

"That's fine."

"The room has four beds in it. Are the English girls with you?"

"No, but they need a place to sleep. You could tell they were English?"

"When you meet as many foreigners as I do it isn't difficult to tell them apart."

"It's a talent. How's your father?"

"Eighty-two this winter. He still talks of the afternoon you drank wine together."

"May he celebrate it and live long for you," Stephen made use of a common Greek expression. "Does he still have my envelope or did he burn it like I suggested?"

"Safe in his shop. My son is bringing sheets and blankets; shall I have him get it for you?"

"No, I'll be seeing your father. So where's this room? I'll explain the situation to the girls."

"This way."

Renas led them up the few remaining steps to the town but turned left before entering it down a slippery path. The lighting was sparse and, though he could make his way in complete darkness, he slackened his pace to point out unseen steps or drops or animal dung to be circumnavigated.

"Where are we going?" asked Nancy.

"To see a room," said Stephen. "He has only one vacancy but it has four beds. If it's agreeable we can all stay there tonight and find other accommodations tomorrow. It's late and it'd be difficult to locate other landlords. If you don't want to stay there I'll take you to the tourist police. They may know of other vacancies."

"Let's see what it's like," said Jill, "tonight all we need is a bed."

"But we don't know Stephen," said Nancy.

"For God's sake Nancy, what do you imagine he'll do, ravage or murder us in our sleep?"

"It's a possibility," said Stephen.

"No, but..." Nancy paused. "Well, where is this room exactly and what will it cost?"

"We'll know where it is when we get there," said Stephen. "It will cost us thirty drachmas apiece and seven extra for a shower."

"It's less than we were paying on Ios," Jill observed.

"From here," said Renas.

They filed after him under the lintel of a doorless doorway that gave access to no building to ascend four steps and descend three more. Turning a corner they found themselves in a rectangular, cement courtyard. Lengthwise, on the left it was confined by a bare wall and on the right by a bathroom and two adjacent rooms. On the back wall was the entrance to the room that Renas had brought them to inspect.

It was a deep, windowless room, cool and clammy and streaked with moisture. The ceiling was curved in the shape of an arch. Renas clicked on the light switch and the bulb suspended at the end of a coiled yellow cord glistened a milky tincture off the walls.

"It's so musty in here," said Nancy.

"It's the altitude. At night every place up here is damp," said Stephen.

"And chilly."

"Tell her my son is bringing blankets," Renas reminded Stephen when Nancy removed a shawl from her knapsack, "two for each of you. With them sleeping is very comfortable."

Except for four metal beds, one in each corner, the room was devoid of furnishings. On the back wall was a chipped sink and mirror. Renas screwed on the faucet and drank some water with his free hand.

"You see, it is pure," he said, drying his mouth with his palm, "drinkable unlike the shower water. It has its own tank. Of all my rooms only this one has a sink like this. Tell them for me."

Stephen relayed the room's attribute as directed. Dropping his bags on the bare mattress to the left of the door, he asked Renas to have that bed made up for him.

"I'm going to wash up," he said to Jill. "Decide while I'm gone what you want to do. I want to get something to eat before the taverna closes."

Outside the stars and quarter moon were crisply visible in the sky. Outside a cockroach waddled toward its den. The girls would stay the night.

"Sure?" Stephen looked to Nancy.

"Positive," said Jill. "Could we go with you to get something to eat? We're both famished."

"Of course. Where's Renas?"

"Don't know. Gone. He left us this key."

"Does he know which beds you plan to sleep on?"

"The ones beside our packs," said Jill, propping hers against the bed across from Stephen's.

CHAPTER 4

The taverna faced April 21 Street. Light poured out of the windows onto the pavement in uneven pools. Inside it was laden with the commingled aroma of olive oil and herbs and sauces. Its off-white walls were spotted with grease. Along the back wall behind a glass counter, above a passageway to the kitchen and smaller dining area, ran a shelf of wine bottles the length of the room. One customer, a girl in her early twenties, sat knitting and blowing the steam off a cup of coffee. She had a round face and short curly dark hair and disconsolate eyes. Jill nodded to her before joining in the occupation of a square wooden table by the counter.

"What shall we have?" Jill wondered, dusting an earlier customer's bread crumbs onto the floor.

"Translate the menu," said Nancy, pushing it toward Stephen, "it's in Greek. You speak the language, can you read it?"

"Don't have to," he said.

"You mean you can't?"

"I mean at this hour we'll have to eat whatever's left in the kitchen."

"Macaroni and *soudzoukakia*," the knitting girl broadcast that she spoke English.

"What's sukiya?" asked Nancy. "It sounds Japanese."

"*Soudzoukakia*," Stephen repronounced, "spiced meatballs in tomato sauce."

"I want a salad," said Jill.

"A village salad with tomatoes and cucumbers and feta cheese and Kalamata olives and anchovies and..."

"Brilliant," said Jill.

"Wine," Stephen concluded.

"I'd prefer beer," said Nancy.

"But I want to buy you wine. Humor me."

"I'm not partial to wine."

"You'll like this one."

A young woman emerged from behind the counter. She did not receive new customers with enthusiasm. At first, she tried to ignore them in the hope they would leave. When they did not, she condescended to take their order. She returned to the kitchen and a busboy appeared in her place carrying a tray with water glasses filled with silverware and napkins, three small wine glasses, a basked of bread and a bottle of white *Domestica*.

"It's customary in Greece to say *aspro pato* and drink down the first glass of wine," said Stephen.

"*Aspro pato*," and the click of two glasses.

"*Aspro pato*," click, click.

The wine was cold and refreshing.

"It's quite good," said Nancy.

"The let's do it again." Stephen suggested.

"Not again."

"It will make you feel good."

"I already feel good."

"Then it will make you feel better. I tell you what, we'll drink to something. How 'bout trust?"

"To trust," said Jill, "*aspro pato*."

Nancy raised her glass reluctantly but drank it down.

The village salad was deposited in the middle of the table and all ate directly from it. They dunked their bread in the olive oil that remained in the bowl and washed it down with wine until the bottle was empty and Stephen ordered another.

"So your name is Stephen," Jill said, stretching forward to light her cigarette on his match. "Where are you from?"

"Thoreau said home is where you sit."

"So you're from that chair," said Nancy.

"How do you like my home?"

"Charming, now be truthful," said Jill.

"Why? My past if of no consequence to me so why should it be to you?"

"Curiosity."

"What do you do?" Nancy asked. "To live I mean."

"Drink your wine."

"Alright, but answer."

"I don't."

"You don't what?"

"I don't live."

Nancy was in the process of draining her glass of its wine. She bent back her head and made a show of its emptiness by holding the glass upside down a few inches above her open mouth.

"I tried to warn you but you wouldn't listen," she said to Jill. "We're sharing a room with one of those living dead."

"Yes," Jill took it up, "and who only comes out at night to nourish himself on the blood of young virgins."

"The only kind I ever touch," Stephen played along.

"Speaking for myself, you're out of luck but I would never presume to swear about Nancy's condition."

"Enough," Nancy pushed her glass to the center of the table, her cheeks noticeably flushed from the wine," where's the bloody suki-whatever?"

The *soudzoukakia* and second bottle of wine were being served by the young woman as a swollen-legged man in his seventies shuffled into the taverna. He was heavy set; with large forearms that made him appear stronger than his aging body. His face wore the white stubble of a day's growth of beard and his eyes looked death invaded. He made a gesture of recognition to the young woman who ignored him and continued tidying unoccupied tables. Undaunted by her reaction, he continued into the room pausing to exchange a few words with the knitting girl. They conversed amicably in Greek until he spotted Stephen who was too involved with his dinner to take notice of anyone else.

"Eh, *yassou file*, hello friend," he said gregariously, "when did you get back?"

"On the last ship from Athens," Stephen mumbled through a mouthful of macaroni.

"It's good to find you here. Just this morning Renas and I were speaking about you. It was a kind thing you did for him last summer."

"It was nothing I did for him. Come and help me with this wine."

The old man did not need to be coaxed. He collected a clean glass from the countertop on the way.

"You're young ladies won't mind the company of a useless old man?" he asked, settling into a wicker-seat chair.

"They're not my young ladies and they're free to leave whenever they wish."

"Time is death, so short. Enjoy yourself while you're young," he patted Stephen's back. "There is nothing in life worthwhile except being squeezed by a young lady's legs."

"That simple is it *levende?*"

Stephen received no reply from the old man who had been introduced to him the previous summer as the owner of the taverna. Stephen called him *levende,* a cordial appellation like *filé* that act as convenient substitutes for forgotten names.

"*Aspro pato,*" said Jill to be noticed.

"*Aspro pato,*" the old man toasted, then asked Stephen how she had come to learn those words.

"I never asked her."

"She's a good girl. Good girl. Tell her I salute her not with *aspro pato* but with *stin egia sou.*"

"He drinks to your health," Stephen told her.

"How nice," said Jill. "How did he say that?"

"You can compress it to *yassou.*"

"*Yassou,*" Jill reciprocated.

"*Yassou,*" the old man clicked her glass and put the final touches of proper pronunciation on the word before offering a "*yassou*" to Nancy.

"Stephen, I really don't think I can drink it all."

"Just take a sip to be sociable Nancy."

"What troubles her?" the old man leaned forward to find out.

"Too much wine."

"Tell her to put some more food in her stomach," he advised. "What are you eating?"

"Soudzoukakia."

"No. What you need is meat, or lambs intestines, or fried squid."

"We arrived too late."

"Iphigenia," the old man called the young woman who had served them.

"Leave me alone," she said.

"Iphigenia, what do you mean by telling my friend that you only have *soudzoukakia*?"

"That's all we have."

"Iphigenia," the old man implored.

"Leave me alone. I work hard all day and it is late. If they wanted something else they should have come earlier."

"They just arrived. Be ashamed girl. Hospitality. Hospitality."

"All day long all I do is cook and take orders, cook and take orders, cook and wash dishes. It's fine for you who do nothing all day to expect to be waited on half the night."

"I only want a little meat," the old man lifted his arms in a gesture of innocence.

"Then cook it yourself."

"Never grow old," he grumbled to Stephen. "Never marry, it leads to children whether you want them or not. Stay young and free like a bird. Live the way your heart tells you. I work hard raising a daughter, I arranged the marriage of her choice, I gave her this taverna for her dowry and how am I repaid? With a son-in-law that smells like his mules and a 'cook it yourself'."

"We take care of you," said Iphigenia.

"In my house."

"In the house that was my mother's dowry."

"Eh, you make me sorry I ever loved your poor mother."

"This fuss is over nothing," said Stephen. "The *soudzoukakia* were filling."

"Listening to her you would think I had done something horrible to her as a child. But you will have some fruit? Yes? And I'll get it myself," he shouted.

"No," said Iphigenia. "You'll make a greater mess for me to clean. I'll get it."

"Apple, grapes, cantaloupe, watermelon," he ordered.

"Whatever we have."

"And another bottle of wine," he winked at Stephen. "And walnuts with honey, I remember you liked that from last year. But I must help her. She will take all night if I'm not there to encourage her."

"Where's he going?" Jill asked.

"To get some fruit and wine."

"No more wine," Nancy turned over her empty glass. "Who is he?"

"He used to own this place but now it belongs to his daughter."

Enough history. Stephen felt too good to have his mood spoiled by a barrage of questions. Looking beyond Jill, he saw the knitting girl set her work aside.

"Join us for some fruit and wine?" he asked her in English.

"No thank you."

"Why? What did an apple ever do to you?"

"Nothing."

"Well?"

"Maybe for some fruit."

Good, Stephen thought, they can give her the third degree and let me be.

"This is Nancy and Jill and my name is Stephen."

"Esther," she said.

Esther was slightly plump in a halter top and shorts. Stephen sat back to observe the proceedings.

"I couldn't help overhearing Kyrie Thori and his daughter..." Esther began.

Thori, Thori, Thori, Stephen would remember his name.

"You arrived tonight?"

"Yes," Nancy confirmed, still deciding how to react to Esther's presence.

"Where are you from?

"Are from or came from today?"

"Both."

"Are from England, came from Ios."

"It's a beautiful island."

"Very," said Jill. "We were only going to spend one day there and ended up staying three."

"I know that feeling," said Esther, beginning to feel at ease. "I'm from Canada, Quebec, and have been living on Santorini since last October."

"Have you found work here?"

"A boyfriend."

"Same difference," Nancy observed.

"Sometimes I think so. His father owns the Hotel Atlantis down the street and a tourist shop in the next block that Laki manages. What do you do?"

"We're in our final year at university," said Jill.

"And you?" Esther asked Stephen.

"A good question," said Nancy. "We think he's American and, oh before I forget, is there a hotel at one of the beaches?"

"Yes, but you can't stay there now."

"Why not?"

"It's near the excavation site at Akrothiri," Esther explained. "Archaeologists discovered a Minoan city there. This is the Lost Continent of Atlantis."

"Some people were discussing it on the ship today," Jill recalled.

"When there's a dig the archaeologists rent out the hotel. It's not very large and a group of them are here. The city they're unearthing was preserved in lava."

"Lava?"

"Didn't you know, Santorini is a live volcano?"

"No, we didn't," said Nancy.

"Be brave," said Stephen.

"I shall be thank you very much. And I'll have some more wine."

"Move, move," the old man chased the busboy out from behind the counter, traipsing on his heels. "Clear the table then bring another bottle of wine. Make sure it's cold. Behold," he laid down an oblong platter of cleaned fruit. "I apologize, no walnuts."

Personifying the spiritual resiliency of old age Kyrie Thori, at times humorous, at times philosophical, always vociferous, was a unique host. Unsure about how to react to him, he mesmerized Nancy and Jill who became putty in his hands. He used Stephen as an intermediary. Through him, he pampered the girls, cajoled them into dunking slivers of apple in wine before eating them and then scolded them for doing the same with other fruit. He imitated their sacrilege and then forgave them. He told them they were beautiful and taught them to drink a glass of wine by lifting it solely with their teeth. For an encore, he pinched the top end of a glass with his thumb and index finger and poured the wine neatly down his gullet. The latter was a feat that Nancy tried to emulate and won for her efforts a coughing fit and a wet chin.

Chapter 5

It was past midnight before Stephen was able to bring the gathering to a natural conclusion. Stephen assured Thori that he would be happy to let Jill and Nancy stay on except they would be unable to find their way back to the room and they were tired and it was late and there would be tomorrow. Esther, who had seemed preoccupied and apart from the group, was quick to second Stephen's allusion to time and the need for sleep. Since she traveled in the opposite direction, the trio parted company with her outside the taverna with an invitation to go swimming with them tomorrow.

"If I can," she said in a rush. "I'll have to check with Laki. I usually help him with the shop. Why don't you drop by in the morning?"

The wind had perked up and was rattling loose doors and shutters. Stephen and Jill huddled together using their bodies as a windbreak to light their cigarettes. Nancy strolled ahead of them, turning in circles to keep them in view.

"Which way?" Nancy asked at a crossroad of alleys.

"Wait for us," said Jill.

"No, it's too bloody cold."

"Left," Stephen directed.

The alley of downward stairs was barely three feet wide and black as a sunless cavern. Nancy moved slowly, bracing herself by running her palms along the buildings on either side of her. She measured the depth of each step like a cautious bather testing the sea's temperature before risking a plunge.

"Why are we taking this path?" she shouted up to Stephen and Jill, imagining she had put more distance between them than she had. "We didn't before."

"Not so loud," Stephen led Jill into the darkness. "I think it's a shortcut."

"It's a tunnel. I like it. Do you really think that it was his son-in-law's mules Jill and I rode up the cliff?"

Stephen had stopped to kiss Jill. She responded and he kissed her again and slipped his hand underneath her sweater and discovered she wasn't wearing a bra. That stiffened him and she felt it against her thigh.

"Well?" Nancy leaned against the wall to await her answer.

"Maybe," he said.

"How did he put it again?"

"That it was likely his mules but one could have been his son-in-law incognito because of a distinct family resemblance between them."

Nancy laughed as uncontrollably over Stephen's repetition of Thori's attitude toward his son-in-law as she had in the taverna. She laughed until a hissing "Shhh" from the window beside her startled her into a scream. She jumped back against the opposite wall, blindly searching for the angry voice that seemed to accost her out of nowhere.

"Bloody bastard, bloody bastard," she cursed in defense.

"What's the matter, did you trip?" asked Jill. "Are you hurt?"

"A bloody bastard tried to frighten me to death."

"Just keep going," said Stephen.

"The bloody bastard."

"She's had too much to drink," said Jill. "We better catch her up."

They hurried out of the dark alley onto the path that ran along the cliff's edge. Light reflected up from Rue Marinatos. Nancy was resting against the low stone parapet gazing down at where the sea must somewhere have bottomed the darkness. A vaporous cloud wafted up from below by a draft of wind gave the impression of smoke.

"I thought the volcano was on fire," she said. "Mystical?"

"How do you feel?" asked Jill.

"Tired. That voice scared me so my heart's still racing. And my ears are buzzing. Is the room much farther?"

"No," said Stephen, "that was a shortcut."

Stephen supported Nancy the rest of the way with an arm about her waist. They were home in little time. The bulb above the community bathroom remained on at night to light the courtyard and Jill searched her bag beneath it for the key to their room. She unlocked the door and entered first to switch on the light. The designated beds had been made up with coarse white sheets and pillow cases. Two woolen blankets were folded in quarters at the foot each bed. Nancy released herself from Stephen and moved unsteadily to the one nearest the sink by her knapsack.

"Stephen, kindly wait outside while I undress," said Nancy. "I don't believe I could make it to the loo and back."

In exile, Stephen paced the courtyard's dimensions until he came across a flight of stairs beside the bathroom and climbed them. On the flat roof, the water storage tank for the shower was being drummed by the wind. In daylight, Stephen could have scanned half the town. In the dark, he could hear the rustle of a tree in a neighbor's garden and the doleful moaning of two cats. Remembering a joint a friend in Athens had given him for his trip in his jacket pocket; he found a place to sit and lit it.

"I thought you might be up here," said Jill, peering over the last stair.

"Nancy?"

"Sound asleep."

"Care for some?" he showed her the joint.

"Please," she sat down beside him. "I haven't had any since we left England."

He watched her inhale the smoke and squint her eyes as though to draw more potency into her lungs. With her free hand she wound her fingers through his shoulder length straight, brown hair, curling it about her finger of the back of his neck.

When she exhaled she unwound her fingers and offered back the joint.

"If Nancy was here…there's never been a voice for her own morality since…" Jill scoured her mind for the right allusion but came up blank.

"Why?"

"Who can say? And she can be so obnoxious and stubborn. I was shocked that she agreed to sleep in the same room as you. And the way you and the old man made her drink wine," Jill laughed. "She never drinks wine."

"She's your friend isn't she?"

"Not exactly," she held the joint toward Stephen. "I don't want anymore."

"Then put it out and save the rest if you want."

Jill smudged it out making sure not to lose any leaves.

"Nancy's an acquaintance. We share a flat in Brighton with two other girls who also attend Sussex. One of them is a friend since grammar school. She was supposed to spend this holiday with me but her mother was placed in hospital three days before our departure. Moira would have been so much fun to travel with but she couldn't leave her mother. Nancy had been living with us for some months and when she agreed to take her place I was even ecstatic. I didn't fancy spending a month alone in a foreign country, well France maybe but not Greece. So I've been here a fortnight that Nancy's made seem like two years; always bickering about where to go and who we can speak to, well you've seen what she's like."

Stephen kept his silence.

"What can I do? We're not friends but we're school mates. She tempts me but I'm not adventurous enough to risk being alone. Do you know, this is the most enjoyable night I've spent in Greece, the first night I haven't regretted coming."

"I'm glad you did."

Stephen brought Jill's mouth to his. Her lips were easily coaxed open. His fingers traced the shape of her breast and he physically ached for her.

"No. It's chilly isn't it?" she said and stood to straighten her sweater. "I'm so sleepy. Thank you for the..." she jiggled the remains of the joint in her fist. "How long do you intend to stay out here?"

"A while."

Stephen made no attempt to conceal his disappointment. He ignored Jill as she left.

Tomorrow I get rid of them, he decided. One's a virgin and the other thinks she can keep me interested by feeding herself to me a morsel at a time. If you're here for a reason, remember it.

He couldn't get the gaunt image of the old man on the ship out of his mind, so white among all those tan faces, trying to complete the journey to his gravesite alive, telling Stephen that youth was all there was to life. If that was so, why had the old man lived as long as he had?

I won't live that long, he reassured himself, but he knew he could not be sure how long he would drag it out. At twenty-three he already felt old. The relentlessness of age overwhelmed him each time he contemplated the universe and its infinite size. It expanded with every second of thought and he could feel himself shrink to insignificance until all hope and hope for meaning was lost.

"Enough," he put an end to it and returned through the courtyard to the room.

Stephen undressed in the dark and clumped his clothes in a bunch on the peg beside the door. He groped his way to bed and slipped between the clammy sheets. Jill was beside him. He could feel the warmth of her breath and her naked body press up against him.

"I thought you meant no," he whispered.

"Did you? Perhaps I changed my mind. Now be nice, don't talk and spoil it by waking Nancy."

Jill was eager and uninhibited and moist after the first kiss. She knew how to use her legs and thighs without disturbing the bed and they enjoyed each other twice with Stephen stifling her moans by covering her mouth with his hand or kisses.

TUESDAY

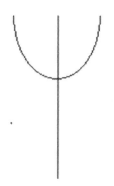

CHAPTER 6

STEPHEN WOKE WITH THE STALE taste of wine in his mouth. He was alone in the hot room and his sheets were soaked with perspiration. Turning on his side, he wrestled the blanket to the foot of the bed. His arm was numb and he felt the effervescent tingle of blood circulate through it. A line of humid light seeped beneath the door. The phlegmatic atmosphere would have seduced him into a complacent slumber had the door not opened and flooded the floor with sun.

"Wake up lazy," Jill nudged him playfully.

Nancy followed her into the room. Both wore short, loose cotton dresses and they sat on the bed across from and him he could see their thighs.

"Do you always sleep this late? Jill and I have already toured the town. Fantastic metamorphosis. So high above the sea. Would you like to see what we bought?"

Nancy elevated a package of brown, twine-fastened paper from Jill's lap and ripped it apart.

"Sandals from Laki's shop. Esther made him give us a special price."

"I need a cigarette," said Stephen.

"It's not good to smoke on an empty stomach."

"I'll get it," said Jill.

She used it as an excuse to sit on the bed with him. Nancy huddled over in narcissistic admiration of her perfect feet and how they looked in her new footwear.

"Esther can't go to the beach," she said. "Laki's expecting a tour boat and customers and she wants to help out at the shop. I think it was a convenient excuse."

"What do we care? We're still going aren't we Stephen?" Jill assumed rather than asked.

For giving yourself to me last night that much I owe you, Stephen thought. That and nothing else.

"What's the time?" he asked.

"Going on ten."

"We should get going. You can wear your bathing suits or gamble on finding a tree to change behind. Have you had breakfast?"

"Jill insisted on waiting for you for some reason," Nancy complained.

CHAPTER 7

A strong sun glared off the white-washed buildings. Aside the breezy parapet Stephen could see the sapphire hues of sky and sea consummate their union and make the linear horizon finite. Like a painted pane of glass, the silent sea swept back from the cliff to surround the crater island of the volcano that waits, an unassuming Phoenix, for the season to destroy itself and be reborn.

The bus to Kamari beach made three trips a day at eleven, two and five, or there about. Stephen informed the girls of that fact and that there were no places to eat at the beach. They decided to make an outing of the excursion by carrying food and staying by the shore until evening. He did not object to their plan for the same reason he had not opposed Jill's inclusion of him in their day. That reason had less to do with her having given herself to him and more with his belief that on any Greek island there was no better way to celebrate one's arrival than inactive by the shore listening to the waves. It was an insular effect of the country that drove him to the sea for distraction as though it cradled some secret to be revealed to him alone.

Food would be bought in the town and wine from their landlord's father. It would afford Stephen the opportunity to pay his respects to the wine merchant the islanders called "Barba" in deference to his age.

Off Rue Marinatos, they found old man Trekas in a wicker chair outside his shop. He was reading a newspaper he had folded down to palm size, shooing a fly that kept landing on his arm in search of bacteria. He seemed happy to see Stephen and invited the trio in out of the sun.

Entering from the stark sunlight, the one room shop was oppressively dark, like a monk's cell at Meteora. It reeked with the dry, vinegary odor of spilt wine. Nearly every foot of space was cramped by wooden barrels and oversized bottles that covered the walls and overflowed onto the floor. It was difficult to stand, let alone sit, as Barba insisted. He rummaged through the shop for chairs and up came with two that he passed over a barrel to Stephen. He would have brought in the one from outside had Stephen not convinced him of the brevity of their visit.

"You say hello and good-bye in the same breath," Barba only spoke Greek.

"I'm sorry," said Stephen, "but I don't control the busses."

"Yes, yes. Have you time for a cup of coffee?"

"No. I only stopped by to see you."

"Renas told me you were back. Did he give you a good room?"

"Of course."

"He is a good boy."

"Good man."

"Yes, but a father's son is always his boy no matter how manly he becomes. God willing you will discover that for yourself. When that day comes, I hope you will be as fortunate as me. Or do you have such intentions with one of these pretty girls?"

"Just friends."

"A husband and wife should be friends. It is the most essential ingredient in marriage; more than love because it brings respect. You should find a wife Stephanos. It would give you a new perspective. It is the way God means man to live. They don't understand Greek?"

"No."

"Good. If a foreign girl is not exactly what you desire," he rocked his head, "you know you can trust old Barba. We have some ripe virgins in the villages here about. For you I could get one that would be both beautiful and," he rubbed his fingers seriously, "bring a dowry. I have in mind my niece's daughter Zoe…"

Stephen cut short Barba's ramblings after the girl's name which was incidentally the Greek word for *life*.

"Tomorrow you can arrange my life with Zoe but today I need a bottle of wine for the beach."

"Your life with Life eh," Barba laughed at the play on words. "Wine, why not? What kind do you like?" he asked Nancy, stooping over to pat her knee.

Nancy looked to Stephen but Barba was already taking down a sampling glass and filling it with one barrel's red wine and offering it to Jill.

"He wants you to taste it," said Stephen.

Barba stroked Jill's cheek while she drank as though fondling a child.

"This one is a *kukla*, doll," he told Stephen.

"Too sweet," she decided.

"Let me," Nancy swept the glass into her hand. "Too, too sweet."

The final verdict was reserved for Stephen. He finished the wine Nancy had left him and said diplomatically,

"It's good Barba but not for the beach."

"Just what do you want?" he sounded a bit disappointed.

"That incomparable white wine of yours."

Incomparable perk the old man's ego.

"Certainly."

How could he have forgotten how much Stephen liked his white wine? Hadn't he taken two bottles back to Athens with him last summer? He must be getting old if he could not remember his customers' preferences.

All of Barba's wines were made from grapes cultivated on Santorini. He was ever anxious to proclaim that the island's rich ash soil, so conducive to the production of wine grapes, was the volcano's peace offering. To him the volcano was not a brute, unjust force but an old man like himself who, frustrated beyond his will at times, let off a little steam. The major eruption of 1957 that destroyed many of Thira's picturesque Venetian villas and Byzantine churches was forgiven by Barba when he found his wine shop miraculously undamaged. Not a wine bottle had been shattered by the fissure, not a barrel had been split open. That had been a sign that he was right.

"Here," he said to Stephen after inspecting several quart bottles in straw casings, "the one you like, and a corkscrew. You can return it later. I may not be here but you know where I hide my key."

Incomparable: that was a good word.

CHAPTER 8

Stephen had expected to breakfast in the café on April 21 Street but its glass doors were chained and padlocked. A sign had been taped to one of its windows that read: "Closed by order of" an illegible name.

"He should have stayed in bed, who knows what it will cost him in business," a vendor was addressing a group of men, "and on a day when the tour ship passes through."

"What happened?" Stephen asked.

"The owner tried to charge a French couple twenty-five instead of two point five drachmas for a cup of coffee and they called the tourist police," one man explained.

"And yet," the vendor injected, "he would have been let off with a reprimand had his mother not called the French girl a prostitute and police imbeciles. That was too much."

"What did they do to him?"

"Locked him up for the day," said the vendor as though that was the natural punishment to be proscribed for such an offense.

Consequently, Stephen and the girls went directly to the marketplace to purchase cheese and tomatoes and sandwiches for lunch and pomegranates and blood oranges and a bottle of mineral water. From there they went to the empty plaza at the back of the town to await their bus. They discovered another café with two tables set out on the sidewalk and ordered three coffees. Across the way, a kite rose up from behind a carpenter's shop. Nosing its progress against the wind, when it achieved a certain altitude it serenely floated in a pocket of air as though defying any string to prevent its escape. The moment it became a fixture in the sky, a Mercedes bus bore into the square, horn blaring, kicking up a cloud of dust.

Out of everywhere, a throng of people siphoned toward the bus. Most were children and kerchiefed women in long, dark dresses. The girls were able to squeeze on board in time to claim two seats. Stephen was swept by the push to the front of the bus.

Although it was possible to see the sea as soon as the bus pulled out of the plaza, it took half an hour to reach the beach. The road looped and curved down the back slope of the island and made frequent stops at innocuous intersections of dirt paths, ravines and solitary olive trees to discharge passengers. The pavement ended abruptly at the shore by a mud-brick wall.

Across the rutted road, a scattering of Cyprus and poplar trees, loud with crickets, extended along the barren landscape. Stephen and the girls crossed the vibrating bridge of shadows formed by their interlocking branches onto the wide, flat beach of black sand. A boulder jetty, congregated by Greek boys, severed the long shore.

Nancy's insistence on privacy prompted the trio up the beach out of sight and sound of other bathers. They spread their towels in the warm sand by the trees and folded their clothes in the cool shade.

"It looks delicious," Jill said about the sea. "What are we waiting for? I'm ready for a swim."

"You two go," said Nancy, adjusting the strap of her bikini.

"She's embarrassed because she can't swim," said Jill.

"I'm not."

"Come on," Jill took Stephen's hand.

The water was colder than it looked on its sun-sparkled surface. Stephen swam ahead of Jill until she called out that she wanted to return.

"Delicious," she reaffirmed after trying to scoop up a silver fish.

"Then why did we come out so soon?"

Stephen sat down with her in the sand.

"To get Nancy. If I don't encourage her she'll never get wet."

"Is it so important to you?"

"Not important."

Jill reclined on her elbows. She turned her face to the wind and closed her eyes with pleasure. Stephen thought how her breasts seemed even fuller in the sun.

"Nancy," her voice rang out above the surf.

"I'll send her down to you."

"Don't you want to go in again?"

"Later."

"Tell Nancy if she isn't quick I'll bring some water and douse her."

Nancy had moved under the trees. She greeted Stephen with the offer of an extra towel.

"The sun will dry me. Why are you in the shade?"

"I burn easily."

"Jill wants you to go in for a swim."

"Why's it black?" Nancy asked about the handful of sand that sifted through her fingers.

"Because thirty-five hundred years ago the volcano covered the island with lava and ash. Her parting words to me were if Nancy can't go to the sea the sea shall come to her."

"I heard her. Getting me wet is a ritual she performs each time we go to the beach. I hoped it might be different today with you here. I suppose if I'm to get wet anyway I might as well appease her."

"Take the wine and water bottles with you. Put them in the sea to cool."

Stephen stretched out on his towel, back to the sky. It was soothing to lie in the hot sun made bearable by blows of breeze that could be heard penetrating the treetops. All he could see were the immediate mounds of sand. Concentrating on individual grains, they became a universe of infinitesimal worlds disheveled by a temperate wind into unenvisioned patterns. His body deserted him. He became his eyes. The little they could see became all that existed. His eyelids closed and all that existed became an orange red color that darkened into gray whenever a passing cloud obstructed the sun.

CHAPTER 9

"He's going to burn," said Nancy.

Stephen felt a cool hand on his shoulder.

"No, he's tan," said Jill, "and his hair is down to…"

"Still."

"Did we wake you yet," Jill whispered in his ear. "Are you hungry?"

Stephen turned over on his back and looked into Jill's eyes.

"You are," he said.

"I'll get the wine."

Stephen shook the sand from his towel and removed it to the shade. With the girls' it completed a triangle about the bag containing their lunch. Jill returned with the wine and water. Her feet were sore from the hot sand and she sat to rub the sting from their soles. Nancy distributed the sandwiches while he uncorked the jug of wine.

"It's beautiful here," said Jill, sipping her first glass.

"Where are the other beaches?" Nancy asked between bites.

"On the southern part of the island; but this is the only one with sand."

"I know Thira's behind but what's to the north?"

"Some villages. I've never been to that part of the island. I've been told the peasants aren't fond of strangers. Xenophobes."

"Intriguing," said Jill, "perhaps we should visit them."

"Do busses run there?" asked Nancy.

"One of the island's two part way, there's no paved road to them."

"I wonder what kind of experience could have affected a body of people to so distrust outsiders."

"If any did," said Jill.

"Why say that?"

"You complicate everything Nancy. Maybe they don't like strangers because they just don't like strangers."

"Pomegranate?" Stephen nipped the disagreement.

"How do you eat them?"

"Press the skin with your thumbs. You'll hear the bubbles of pulp pop inside them. When the entire skin's soft, bite into it and suck out the juice. When it becomes dry, squeeze it and suck out some more."

"Until your oral fixation is satisfied," said Nancy.

"I never thought of it that way but if it makes you happy."

"What will it taste like?" asked Jill.

"Sweet if it's good."

Stephen handed each a pomegranate. He lit a cigarette, drank another swig and lay back on his towel. For a while they were quietly absorbed with their fruit.

"Is Santorini the Lost Continent of Atlantis?" Nancy broke the silence.

"It is and it isn't," said Stephen. "What makes you ask?"

"Esther and her boyfriend swear it is," said Jill. "Laki's father even named his hotel the Hotel Atlantis."

"There's a Hotel Atlantis on Crete too."

"Then Santorini isn't Atlantis."

"It's more complicated than that."

"So explain it."

"That would resemble work and people don't work on Greek beaches."

"Go on, we've nothing else to do," urged Jill.

"Have you heard of the Minoans?"

"The name's familiar," said Nancy.

"I see we're going to have to do this the hard way. Around 3300 B.C., on the island of Crete fifty miles south of here, Cretan society evolved into what has been labeled the Minoan Civilization."

Stephen juggled his pomegranate to judge the amount of liquid it contained.

"The Minoans were a powerful, seafaring people."

"Hmm," Jill sighed.

"Look, if I'm to go through it…"

"Pardon."

"They forged an empire out of the Aegean islands. Egypt and the Middle East knew them only as traders. Few if any foreign ships entered these waters."

Stephen bit into his pomegranate. The juice gushed into his mouth, warm and sweet.

"The Minoans were an industrious, artistic people. They invented the double blade ax and in their heyday had the greatest navy in the world. They lived without fear of invasion and never fortified their cities."

"This sounds like a myth," said Nancy.

"Doesn't it. At its peak, Minoan Crete had maybe twelve independent cities and the greatest was Knossos. Must have been quite a sight Knossos. It had a multi-storied palace complex with a courtyard and bull ring surrounded by flat-roofed homes and storehouses and administrative offices that formed a labyrinth of narrow alleys."

"Like Thira today," Jill observed.

"Only better planned."

"I think this pomegranate is finished," said Nancy.

"It isn't," said Stephen. "Squeeze it again until more of the bubbles pop and it's soft then turn it over and bite a hole in the opposite side. But be careful not to drip any juice on your clothes because it stains."

Nancy found a couple of drops on her thigh and rubbed to get them out.

"That doesn't apply to flesh," said Stephen. "Anyway, the Minoans were a life-loving people. They decorated their walls with colorful murals, clusters of flying birds and swimming dolphins and bare-breasted women. They traded with other parts of the world and either developed or acquired a form of writing. There, now you know who the Minoans were."

"That doesn't explain Atlantis," said Jill.

"True. About 1450 B.C. Santorini erupted, perhaps the worst natural catastrophe on the planet since man's existence. The concussion was felt in Egypt."

Stephen watched the girls bite into their pomegranates. Nancy made a small incision and sucked the juice out carefully; Jill bit a hole in hers and used her tongue to make it larger.

"There were warning tremors and the Minoans on Santorini evacuated to Crete to wait it out. Then came the explosion. On Crete, the earth shook and buildings crumbled. Before they could take it all in the tidal wave, a mile high at its peak, flooded out the cities along the northern coast. That was followed by a rain of burning cinders. There was so much soot in the sky that for two days it blackened out the sun. They must have thought it was the end of time."

"Or the Day of Judgment," said Nancy.

"But they weren't Christians expecting one. The Mycenaeans from Greece supplanted the Minoans and they were erased from the world's memory, except in Egypt. In the seventh century B.C. an Athenian named Solon visited Egypt and was shown records by their archivists of a maritime empire they had traded with until it just vanished. Solon brought the story home and his descendent Plato used it in his dialogues and called the lost empire Atlantis. It wasn't his intent to recount the muddled history of the Minoans but to write a myth about a great civilization that was destroyed by the gods when it became immoral and corrupt."

"To draw an analogy with his times," said Nancy.

"He never imagined future readers would interpret it literally. So, like God, Atlantis exists by definition. If you want to believe the Minoans were the Atlanteans then some of them lived here, perhaps swam on this beach and ate pomegranates under trees like these and thought they'd never die."

"Esther said they've found proof that Santorini is Atlantis," said Jill.

"Because archaeologists have uncovered a Minoan center on the southern part of the island at Akrothiri. Like Pompeii, it was preserved by lava so they've found an entire city, not just handfuls of rubble. There are indications that it might have been even more important than Knossos. If it was, and if the Minoan Empire was Atlantis, then Santorini would have been, in a sense, the center of Minoan Civilization and thus the center of Atlantis."

"So, is Santorini Atlantis?" Nancy wanted a definitive answer.

"Of course not," said Stephen. "It's a place that only exists in people's imaginations."

"I prefer Esther and Laki's version," said Jill. "It's simpler."

"Which is?" asked Stephen.

"Santorini is Atlantis period."

"If we put the oranges in the beach bag, we can use the paper bag for our trash," said Nancy.

Stephen took a paperback book from the bag before dropping in the oranges. Lifting his towel, he moved to a nearby tree that he could lean up against.

"Nancy, you're right," said Jill, "there is something erotic about eating a pomegranate. I like it."

CHAPTER 10

Stephen had hardly immersed himself in his book when Jill interrupted him.

"What are you reading?"

He showed her the cover.

"*The Red and the Black,* how clever of you to find a book about red pomegranates and black sand. Put it down and walk with me."

Jill opened her hand to show him the half joint he had given her.

"We could finish it together. Wouldn't that be the afternoon's touch of perfection?"

"I can think of something better."

"Well?" Jill smiled.

"Which way are you walking?"

"To the jetty. I'm lonely for people."

"Make sure you finish smoking it before you get there."

"I'll be careful."

"Going for a stroll?" said Nancy. "I'll keep you company."

"No love, you know how easily you burn."

Jill ran down the sun-baked sand to cool ankle-deep sea. She lit the joint then waved to Stephen before leaving. For the first time that day he wanted her and at that moment and could not take his eyes off her.

"We don't always get along," Nancy felt the need to explain the tone with which Jill had refused her offer of company. "We're different kinds of people."

Stephen kept his eyes on Jill.

"I know the two of you would have enjoyed today much more without me."

Nancy's enunciations of the word *know* struck a nerve.

"Did Jill tell you how we met?"

"You were roommates."

"Flat mates before making this trip. In Brighton we hardly became acquainted. Jill had her schedule and friends and I…"

Stephen wondered why he hadn't noticed that Nancy's eyes were emerald green.

"What I have to say is personal and I don't want it discussed even with Jill."

Here it comes, he thought, she overheard us last night. He gave up on his book and lit a cigarette.

"Then why tell me?" he asked.

"I have to talk to someone. People can't go on indefinitely speaking without ever talking to another person. There was no one in Brighton, not while I lived with Jill and her friends and not during this trip."

She's so self-contained, he thought, even to how she crosses her legs to expose her toes. Whereas Jill exuded sexuality without trying, Nancy held hers in reserve.

"This trip has been a nightmare for me and Jill too, though she blames me for her misery while I fault no one. We're just incompatible. I'm a bit older and experienced than she is and maybe that's why I understand that and Jill can't. Because I'm not like her and her friend Moira, she thinks I'm obstinate and rude and antisocial. Do you? You don't have to answer that, I don't want you to choose sides."

She looked down to her thigh where she studied a sand fly for a prolonged instant before brushing it away. He followed the course of her arm over her small breast and had the sudden urge to bit the flat of her belly just above her bikini to see how she'd react.

"This is embarrassing. I know you're fonder of Jill than me. And you should be. I heard you last night. I couldn't avoid it."

Or let us know, he thought.

"I haven't said anything to Jill or will. But I don't want to overhear things I have no desire or right to hear."

Bitch, he thought.

"Jill came to Greece to have a good time, in every way. She's the right age for it. She hasn't had to look back yet. I came to get away from England and think. Until less than a year ago, I was married. For five years."

"Children?"

"No, he didn't want any. If we had, things might have been different. He was the only man I ever loved and the only one I ever slept with. My life and future made sense. Now, when I try to remember the happiness I felt, there's only confusion and emptiness. I'd never been enough for him, almost from the beginning."

"What happened?"

"Other women. I tried to understand but even he didn't know the answer."

He wanted to fuck other women and they're so available, Stephen thought, simple as that. And if she's as reserved in bed as she seems, he probably tired of her quickly and...

"When he started hitting me and verbally abusing me, I left him. I returned to Sussex to finish my nursing degree, but the students seem so young. I came to Greece but unfortunately I brought myself along. Jill can't relate. I feel weak and vulnerable all the time. I can't cope with men or what they're like at the present. That's why I brought up last night."

Again, he noted.

"Not that I'm sitting in judgment."

"I'm going for a swim," he said.

The abruptness with which he stood up startled Nancy.

"Are you angry with me?"

"Now what reason could I have for being angry with you Nancy?"

"I don't know."

The hell you don't, he thought, you take the unexpected pleasure of a chance encounter and turn it into an embarrassment.

"I shouldn't have confided in you. I thought you'd understand but..."

It felt good to be out in the sun again. It felt good to walk in the sand, hot as it was. It felt best to see Jill coming up the beach toward him.

"Run," he called out to her.

"What?" she shouted back.

"Run."

"I can't here you."

"Run damn it run."

Jill quickened her pace. When she caught up with him, he took her hand and drew her into the sea.

"Hurried for this? The way you called I thought something was happening."

In chest deep sea he kissed her. It was the first time that day that they acknowledged each other as lovers.

"If only Nancy wasn't here," she said.

He pulled her close to him again.

"Don't, we can't and I get excited so easily."

"We could walk to the other end of the beach," he proposed.

"No."

"Why not?"

"I met a couple of blokes by the jetty. Americans. They haven't eaten all day so I invited them to share our oranges. I didn't think you'd mind."

Stephen inhaled a deep breath and dove into the sea. It was an act of ablution. The water was silent and cool and clean. It gave him a euphoric sense of freedom and belonging and he broke the surface with a feeling of strength in his buoyancy and motion. Ahead an interminable seascape drew him like a magnate into its expanse. His focused concentration urged him to swim with confidence without regard to the distance he covered. When he trod water to check his bearings, the shore had shrunk to a pencil line of beach. People were indistinct objects.

He began the long return. But now he could feel the loss of energy expended with each stroke. The muscles in his legs began to tighten and he began to understand the word mortality. He floated, listlessly, to regain his ebbing strength but the invisible current drifted him away from land. When it became apparent that it was a matter of survival, he ignored the pain and pretended that the goal waiting ashore for him was greater than life itself. He started counting each stroke until he became absorbed in their rhythm.

When he reached the shore he was some distance away from the girls, farther up the empty beach. He crawled up onto dry land

and collapsed in the hot sand and rested in the waning afternoon sun.

Chapter 11

In a circle under the trees the four of them lay like a pride of satiated lions. Heaped in the center were the peels of the blood oranges.

"We saved one for you," Nancy held an orange up to Stephen.

"This is Stephen," said Jill.

"Tom," said the larger of the two young men.

"Neal," said the other. "They were good oranges."

The circle expanded to make room for Stephen. Still shaken from his swim, he was in no mood for small talk. Not that he feared death, but he had always assumed that he alone would be the instrument of his own destruction and the sea now caused him to question that assurance. He felt as though his life had been usurped.

"Don't you agree?" Jill appealed to him. "Stephen, you haven't heard a word."

"Agree to what?"

"That Tom and Neal could use our shower without our landlord finding out and charging them."

"Doesn't your place have one?"

"We haven't exactly been staying in a place," smiled Tom.

"More like on one," said Neal.

"We brought sleeping bags with us and have been camping on rooftops at night. The islanders don't seem to mind."

"Except the first night," said Neal.

"What happened?" asked Nancy.

"The owner of the building complained to the police and we had to move," said Tom. "But we found another place near one of the churches and we've stayed there for three days. We could use a shower."

"I don't think our landlord would begrudge you one," said Stephen.

"Then it's settled," said Jill. "Glad you've rejoined the living Stephen. You were gone so long I began to wonder if you'd drowned."

"And if I had?"

"Neal would have eaten your blood orange."

"That so Neal?"

"I've never eaten oranges with red pulp. They're great."

"Catch. I'm still alive but you can have it anyway."

"It's nearing five," said Nancy, "shouldn't we be getting back?"

The girls slipped their dresses over their swimsuits, the men their shirts and jeans. Neal offered to carry the beach bag and wine bottle for the girls.

"We'll be at the bus stop," said Jill and the three set off.

Tall and lanky, Tom got up slowly to help Stephen collect the remaining debris. When they started walking the girls with stout, square-shouldered Neal between them, where still in view.

"That Jill's some chick," said Tom, "beautiful tits. She your old lady?"

"No."

"But you're all staying together."

"I met them last night. We arrived on the same ship."

"What about Nancy? What I'd give to get a grip of her hair. I mean, you got something going on with her?"

"Damn it, they're their own old ladies."

"Sorry man, I didn't mean…"

"I know. Don't worry about it. So what are you and Neal doing on Santorini?"

"We're on our way to India."

"Why?"

"Neal's thinking about becoming a Buddhist."

"Shouldn't you be going to Nepal?"

"You got me. You want to come?"

Stephen laughed.

"What's funny?" asked Tom.

"The way you asked. You sounded like a philanthropist inviting someone aboard his yacht for a cruise."

"It's not that expensive," said Tom. "We brought round-the-world tickets and been doing Europe for six weeks and still have most of our stake. We hitch around and sleep out a lot. Most of our expense is food. Well, what do you say?"

"About what?"

"Going to India."

"Some other time. Why don't you ask Nancy and Jill, maybe they'll go with you?"

"Neal probably has already."

"What are you organizing a crusade?"

"Just looking for people that are good to be with and try to get to know them."

Neal was sitting cross-legged in the sand posed like Siddhartha. The girls were leaning their backs against the mud-brick wall and Tom joined them.

"Neal tell you about India?" Tom asked.

"Uh huh," said Nancy.

"Christ," Stephen muttered to himself, passing by the group to stand alone.

He waged a futile struggle to ignore their presence and convince himself that unlike theirs his life was not ineffectual and absurd. Strangers began to surround him, Greeks with a sprinkling of tourists. He raised his eyes to the sun and prayed: Burn, scorch the hell out of me. But instead of being consumed by fire his vision acquired the rosy tincture of blood oranges. When his pupils normalized to the point of clarity, if what we see is not an illusion, he saw her.

She's the reason I didn't drown, he thought.

She stood across the road, wedged between two young men and their conversation. There was no singular aspect about her to capture a stranger's attention unless one noticed the totality of her beauty. She didn't have breasts like Jill or hair like Nancy or whoever's whatever.

She was looking as despondent as Stephen when her eyes encountered his. There they paused. She smiled at him. It was a subtle smile, one that bystanders would not notice or recognize as a smile. An intimate connection.

Wind disturbed strands of her dark brown hair off her shoulder blowing them across her serenely pretty face. As she smoothed the long strands from her cheek and the corner of her mouth, her friend or lover placed his hand on her hip and drew her into the conversation. She said something to make him laugh then returned her eyes to Stephen. She was tan, wore a white, pullover cotton kaftan that could be bought in any island's tourist shop. Through it could be seen the bottom piece of her bikini, the shape of her modest breast and outline of her nipples and well-proportioned legs. She stood very straight, as though prepared to deflect a caress and concentrated on Stephen. There was timelessness about her; he could imagine her in the ancient *agora* of Athens.

Stephen conveyed the impression that he might approach and her eyes shied away from his. She adjusted her sandal and when she looked up again she timidly avoided looking at him.

The bus arrived. People battled their way aboard. He hoped to find himself close enough to the girl to speak but the bus was overcrowded. Just to breathe was a chore. The girl with her companions wound up in the front while he remained bogged in the middle. Because only a woman and child got off the bus before it reached Thira, he was unable to wend his way forward.

The bus pulled into the plaza. Passengers fought as desperately to get off it as they had to get on. By the time he was able to disembark the girl and her companions had dissolved into one of the alleys.

"Which way?" Neal spoke for the group.

"What are you talking about?"

"How do we get to your place? Showers remember?"

Stephen's response was to start walking. They entered the town from the east. Tom identified the first church they saw as the one nearest the roof he and Neal had appropriated. While they went to collect a change of clothes, Stephen and girls waited for them.

"They're nice," said Jill.

"Who?" asked Nancy, captivated by a puffy cloud.

"The blokes."

"Are they?"

"What are we going to do with the wine bottle and corkscrew?"

"Drop them at Barba's shop, it's on our way," said Stephen.

Tom and Neal returned with a change of clothes and the five walked through the center of town. The tourist shops were reopening for the evening. They descended the top stairs of Rue Marinatos and turned onto the cliff path. The wine shop was locked.

"What now?" Jill set the wine bottle down.

"Our place is just over there," Stephen pointed. "Go on, I'll wait for Barba."

"Why not just leave it on his doorstep?" said Neal.

"If he doesn't return in a few, but you go ahead, we can't all take showers at the same time."

Jill set off and the others followed. When they were out of sight, Stephen located Barba's latch key, unlocked the door and deposited the bottle and corkscrew inside the shop. He locked up and lit a cigarette and sat down on the low wall and dangled his legs over the cliff edge.

Everything is chance, just chance, he mused. I've got to meet her. She can't have left but what if she's leaving the island? No, fate is an ancient brand of existentialism. I'll see her again. I've got to. She may be my last chance. So try, for once try. If it doesn't work then blow your brains out.

The image of the girl was reason for surviving the night. He headed home.

"*Guten tag.*"

"Good day," Stephen reciprocated.

He was not sure who of the two German couples in the courtyard had addressed him. The women, broad-shouldered blonds, were removing bathing suits from the clothes line; the men were loading film in their Lieca cameras.

"I see you met your neighbors," said Tom.

"Yeah," said Stephen

"There's nothing like a large woman."

"You speak German?"

"No need to, we can communicate in other ways."

"Did the old man return?" asked Neal.

"Yes."

Stephen fell onto his bed and rubbed his knuckles on the cool floor. His muscles were beginning to feel the effect of his swim and he felt exhausted.

"The girls decided to shower together to conserve the warm water," said Neal. "Cozy huh? That bathroom's so small you can sit on the toilet while you wash, but man the smell."

"Quit bitching," said Tom, finger combing his thinning hair, "it's better than nothing."

The Germans could be heard conversing.

"Looks like they're off to dinner," said Neal. "How do you say stay away from the boiled octopus in German?"

No reply was offered. The room floated in somnolence. The sun was casting its final streaks like the dying notes of a symphony on a day doomed to extinction.

"Brrrrr."

The girls entered the room with towels wrapped about their heads like turbans.

"There's no hot water in that blasted shower," Jill said, searching for her sweater.

Stephen gathered his towel and clothes and went to bathe.

CHAPTER 12

"We were only in London a few days," Tom was telling Nancy when Stephen returned; Jill and Neal were not there. "It was too expensive so we crossed over to the Continent."

"Then you didn't get a chance to know London," said Nancy. "I love that city. My aunt lives there and I visit every chance I get. It takes time to fall in love with a city. As a tourist you must have spent most of yours at places like St. Paul's, or Westminster, or the Tower."

"We didn't do any sightseeing. We spent most of our time at Oxford Circus going to pubs or playing pinball."

"And you're going to India to study Buddhism?"

Nancy found it incongruous that two prospective students of religion would waste their time at Oxford Circus.

"No. Neal's going there for that, I'm just along for the ride. Besides, we probably won't get there. It's just a destination. Everybody should have someplace to go even if they don't intend to get there don't you think?"

"How long will you keep traveling?"

"Until our money runs out."

"Then?"

"Back home."

"Where's that?"

"Licking County, Ohio."

It didn't occur to Tom that Nancy had no more of an idea where Licking County, Ohio, was than he had of where the Village of Down in Kent might be located.

"I own a farm."

Nancy laughed, "I can't imagine you as a farmer."

"I'm not. It's just twenty acres and I don't cultivate it. I use it as a place to visit and take friends. Most of the time I'm in sunny Miami."

"What do you do there?"

"Work for my brother. He's rock concert promoter and when I need a job he gives me one. He's makes a lot of bread. He just got the South American concession. They're just getting into rock music down there."

"What do you do?"

"Whatever needs doing. Ticket arrangements, hotel reservations, he calls it administrative work on his income tax."

"It must be fascinating to work with musicians."

"It's a business," Tom rubbed the palms of his hands. "When I was young I identified with bands. They were a symbol to me."

"Of what?"

"Change. Like a new day coming. But working with them you learn that it's all about money and drugs and groupies. That's fine but they don't know any more about what's going on then you do. My brother's no better than they are. I remember him when he first got started and all he was going to accomplish. Now it's all dollar signs. There's no such thing as heroes."

"You sound disillusioned," said Nancy. "Why don't you escape your brother's orbit and do something on your own? Work your farm."

Tom grinned, "The money."

The light switched on. Jill and Neal and the night had arrived.

"You sure took your time," Tom said to Neal.

"Have we got news for you," said Jill, sitting down on her bed.

"Good or bad?" asked Nancy.

"Brilliant."

"I returned our things to the rooftop and picked up," Neal cryptically patted his pocket and Tom's eyes acquiesced.

"On our way back we got lost," said Jill. "And just as we found our way, but you tell them Neal."

"We came across a movie theater, if you can call it that,"

"No kidding?" Tom applauded.

"Guess what's playing?"

"It better be good."

"King Kong." Not arousing enthusiasm Neal emphasized, "The original. 1930. With Fay Wray or whatever her name was. The one who did nothing but scream. Show starts at nine which gives us time to eat and get properly prepared."

"Properly prepared?" Nancy looked to Jill.

"Where shall we eat?" Jill ignored her. "How about the place we ate at last night? We met this old gent who got Nancy drunk."

Nancy shook her head, emphatically.

"Then somewhere else."

Chapter 13

They found a *psisteria* on March 25 Street. It sold no prepared foods, only a variety of meats and fish grilled over a charcoal fire. A hole in the ceiling allowed the smoke to escape. There were no windows. The interior's high ceiling and stone floor and wooden beams gave it the appearance of a converted barn. Old photographs in black frames were clustered at various levels on the walls, many positioned to high to make out.

It did a lucrative business, the busboys were busy. Everyone in Stephen's group followed his example and ate lamb chops and fried potatoes and salad and wine. When it came time to pay the bill, the waiter itemized the cost of their feast on the wax paper table cloth.

"Where shall we do it?" asked Neal, after they had left the taverna.

"Do what?" asked Nancy.

He eyed his surrounding and leaned close to Nancy and whispered, "Smoke some hash."

"No."

"Not to worry love, you don't have to participate," said Jill. "We can do it at our place."

"Absolutely not," said Nancy.

"She's right. The Germans might be there and we don't know them," said Neal.

"Why not an after dinner stroll, there's time," said Tom.

They walked through the empty plaza, where the buses were parked, to a grove of olive trees, dark and unmolested by light. In the midst of their contorted trunks and shielding branches, the four of them smoked. Nancy stood apart from them on the pavement to make a point of her disassociation from their activity.

The hash was potent. It concentrated the senses almost immediately and created a mental vacuum that turned consciousness inward. Disturbed time. Made a minute seem to last forever and, when it had passed, seem as though it had been quantitatively foreshortened.

The move theater was a roofless, rectangular room with several rows of folding chairs and more stacked along the rear wall to expand seating capacity. Three Greek youths sat in the back. The pungent odor of their Assos cigarettes permeated the air.

Stephen's group sat toward the front, closer to the painted white square on the yellow wall that served as the movie screen. The sound track was occasionally distorted and the mechanical noise of the projector could be heard throughout the show but the feature started on time.

KING KONG
(Eighth Wonder of the World)
with Greek subtitles

He had to make a movie more exciting and frightening than his last, the film producer told the captain of the freighter he had commissioned to transport him and his technicians to an unchartered island. His public expects it of him. So the Celluloid tale began. Preparations for the voyage were complete, only one detail remained unresolved. But what a detail! A woman had to be found to accompany them. For box office success the producer knew there were two ingredients: adventure and romance. But where would he find her and by midnight? All knowledge-able actresses knew his reputation for recklessness and refused to work for him. He took a taxi into Manhattan. As fate would have it, he came across a young blond out of luck and money. Go with him, he declared, he offered her "money, adventure and fame; the thrill of a lifetime." How could she refuse? Confined for weeks on board the ship, he gave her acting lessons that consisted of expressing fear with her eyes and method screaming, screaming, screaming. She fell in love with the first mate. The island was sighted. The Isle of Skull. Mysterious. Foreboding. A landing was made. The natives were in the midst of a tribal ceremony preparing to offer a young maiden to some creature lurking behind a colossal stone wall built in the shape of a skull. The chief spotted the white men. He was willing to trade the producer some livestock for his blond heroine so that she might be given to the creature in the hope of finally appeasing him. No deal. The shore party returned to the ship. But the natives were not to be dissuaded. That night they slipped aboard and kidnapped her. A second shore party was launched to rescue her. They arrived in time to see her being carried away screaming in the palm of a giant gorilla, King Kong. As Kong escaped with his prize into the rain forest behind the skull wall, the producer and first mate and several crewmen tracked him. They discovered that the rain forest was a primeval world populated with dinosaurs. While the first mate continued his pursuit of Kong, the producer returned for more help and explosives. Meanwhile, the heroine screamed, Kong killed a tyrannosaurus then beat his chest victoriously; the heroine screamed, Kong slew a triceratops then beat his chest victoriously; the heroine screamed, Kong strangled a pterodactyl then, as tensions mounted:

Intermission. A boy with a tray strapped to his chest passed down the aisle offering drinks, chocolate bars, potato chips, pistachios and *passa tempo* for sale.

Stephen had seen the movie before. In his opinion it rated only as a 1930 curio for film historians. The plot was ludicrous, the dialogue moronic and the acting pathetic. But having smoked before the show gave it the one thing it lacked, quality. The Isle of Skull became a symbol for the human mind and dialogue took on double entendre. He imagined himself a member of the ship's crew, choosing to remain forever on the island, befriending the natives, dedicating his life to the investigation of that primordial garden, overcoming all fears, expanding his realm of knowledge. Why did smoking have that effect? The movie had not improved since he had last seen it. Then it dawned on him that what he had enjoyed was not the movie but his own subconscious, in its kef state, triggered by the cinematic images. It could have been any movie. Good or bad it would not have matter.

Stephen bought a bottle of Coca Cola and a bag of *passa tempo*. By the close of intermission he was ankle deep in pumpkin seed shells and no longer high. He paid little attention to the rest of the film: the capture of Kong, his transportation to New York City, his escape and execution atop the Empire State Building by a squadron of biplanes – the end.

"So that was King Kong," said Nancy as the group filed out of the theater.

"I love old movies," said Neal. "What did you think of it?"

Nancy didn't offer an opinion.

"You should have smoked with us," Neal added. "Well, what shall we do next?"

"We could buy a couple bottles of wine and walk down the cliff and drink them by the sea," said Tom.

"And then have to walk back up, no thank you. Bed is more appealing," said Nancy.

"There's a discotheque," said Stephen.

"You sure? We've been here for three days and haven't heard of it," said Tom.

"It was open last year but it might have closed down."

"Where is it?"

Stephen pointed toward the northern part of town.

Chapter 14

"Over there."

They had been walking for ten minutes passed a small museum and a round-walled church.

"Where?" Neal couldn't see it.

"There," Jill took his head in her hands and aimed it toward the entrance.

"The Volcano Discotheque," Neal read the sign.

Inside, to the left of the door, was a booth where drinks were mixed and a shelf that held a stereo system and records. The room was oddly shaped, the left portion of it beyond the bar being deeper than the right. Each section had its own arched roof and at the point where two domes intersected a brass fixture with a mood light had been hung. The walls were decorated with bacchanal scenes of reclining satyrs and nymphs, eating grapes and fornicating by wooded banks of ponds and streams while a volcano smoldered in the background.

A sedate party of five was seated at a table on the right side of the discotheque. Their presence prompted Nancy to claim a table on the opposite wall. Stephen slid down one of the benches ending up with his side against the wall. Jill sat between him and Neal, with Nancy and Tom across from them. The owner, a young man with a jet black moustache, trailed them to the table to take their order.

"I don't want hard liquor," said Tom.

"We could all drink wine," said Jill.

Stephen ordered a bottle for the table and *ouzo* for himself.

"So this is the discotheque," Neal glanced about, "back home it wouldn't even qualify as a bar. There isn't even a dance floor."

"You're on Santorini, an island where everything is different," said Nancy.

The drinks arrived.

Stephen wanted distraction and invited the owner to join them. While he fetched a glass, Stephen poured the wine. When he returned, he passed him a glass and lifted his *ouzo*.

"*Aspro pato*," said the owner and clicked everyone's glass.

"What's he say?" asked Tom.

"Bottoms up," said Jill.

"Not again. Not another last night," said Nancy.

They drank down. The owner refilled the glasses and encouraged them to shoot another.

"Hey, he's pretty free with our wine," said Neal.

"Not ours, mine," Stephen corrected. "This bottle's mine and if I want to spill it on the floor that's cool. Come to think of it, we should spill some on the ground for the dead. For the dead," he said to the owner in Greek and dripped some wine onto the floor.

"For the dead," the owner imitated his example; whether the wine was swallowed or spilt he would be paid.

"Why isn't there any music?" said Tom.

Stephen asked the owner to play some records and bring another bottle and some bread. He finished what wine remained directly from the bottle and handed over the empty.

"What's gotten into you Stephen?" asked Jill, sliding her arm through his.

"I want to get drunk."

"Why?"

"To stop thinking, isn't that why people get drunk?"

A Greek song came over the speaker.

Oh Thanasi died today,
now they're hounding meeeee-eeeeee-eeeee

The waiter set down a plate of bread and uncorked the wine. Stephen swung his leg over the bench to straddle it and lean his back against the wall. He broke off a piece of bread and dunked it in his wine four times for the Father and the Son and the Holy Ghost and the unholy answer. Tom was filling Nancy in on his sky diving exploits; Jill was telling Neal about her life at university and her friend Moira. Stephen pressed the palms of his hands against his eyes to stop thinking.

The song ended. When he opened his eyes, like an apparition, the girl from beach was there. She had been there all along with the party in the other section of the room. With her were the two young men from the bus plus a middle-aged couple. She had been studying Stephen.

Another *Zeibekiko* song began. The one sung by the young girl yesterday on the ship.

It was a tragic story,
he loved without being loved.

I love her, he thought. No. You've never met her and what the hell is love? No, it's the wine and the *Zeibekiko* music. No, it's her. Idiot. It's her eyes and the way they look at you.

The girl's group was settling their bill with the waiter and preparing to leave. He was considering a way to approach her by inviting them over for a drink but once again the girl shied her eyes from him in the folds of her hair and they left.

It was a tragic story,
he loved without being loved.
Now, living unwanted,
it is death he seeks,
it is death he seeks in wine.

Stephen pounded his fist on the table in frustration and startled Nancy.

"What is it?" she asked.

"Nothing."

"You look like there is."

"Here," he poured another round.

"I think you've had enough. We all have."

"Me included," said Tom. "Let's all just sit back and chill."

Stephen sat passively. Each glass of wine only increased his restiveness. His mind wandered without actively thinking.

"Could we get them to play some other music?" asked Neal.

Lacking an interest in explaining *Zeibekiko* music to Neal, Stephen picked up a piece of bread and walked over to the booth.

"Have you got a pencil and a sheet of paper?" he asked the owner.

"Yes," he took them out of a drawer. "Is everything satisfactory?"

"Could you play some American music for the..."

"Certainly."

"And bring me another glass of *ouzo* with one ice cube please."

Stephen sat at the table nearest the door, from where he could not be seen by his companions. He smoothed the paper on the table and took up his pencil. He wanted to focus his thoughts by writing something, anything, but nothing came to mind. Only doodles of stars and numbers. *Jumpin' Jack Flash* came out of the speakers. He thought of the girl and sipped his drink and lost track of time until Neal patted his shoulder.

"So there you are," he said.

"We're ready to leave," Jill sat down beside him. "You draw beautiful stars."

"What do we owe?" Tom asked.

"You go, I'll pay and we can settle up tomorrow. I want to finish my *ouzo*."

"We can wait for you," said Jill.

"No."

"You heard the man," said Neal, winding his arm about Jill's waist and urging her to her feet and toward the door.

"We could get lost," said Nancy.

"You can find our place from the center of town and to get there just follow the path we came on."

At last he was left alone. He placed some bills on the edge of the table.

"Take what we owe you," he said to the owner. "Are you going to close now?"

"Take your time."

Stephen began to write. Kong, Kong, Kong, Kong, Kong. They drove, no stole, no brought, no, no. He turned the sheet over and began again:

Kong
I understand;
they kidnapped you from your world
to make a prisoner of you in their own.

What was beautiful to you
was hideous to them.
What repulsed you
they loved.

Sense became nonsense,
and in the instant
that your nightmare
        became your reality
          they killed you.
For Kong,
        as the Gods are merciful,
Humanity is kind.

There's always the question of when a poem is finished and why. He read it once then crumpled up the sheet of paper and put a match to it and watched it burn to dust in the ashtray.

"Good night," he said to the owner, picking up his change and slice of bread.

"Come again."

"Those people at the other table, do they come here often?"

"Never seen them before tonight. Have you?" he asked the waiter.

"Tourists come and go, who can keep up with them?"

It did not take long for Stephen to realize how badly the alcohol would affect him. No sooner was he outside than he had to support himself on the cliff wall to keep his knees from buckling. The stars swam in dizzy patterns overhead and the stones beneath his feet seemed to liquefy. His stomach turned.

Don't let me be sick, he thought as if in prayer, and I won't ever drink that much again.

He leaned over the cliff wall for the cool updraft to sooth his face. His prayer failed him and his stomach turned. He started walking again. The intermittent pools of darkness were as unsettling as the light. At a breach in the wall, his stomach expelled the rest of the liquid and he began to feel better. He ate the piece of bread he carried in his pocket while he walked then lit a cigarette to clear his head.

He had decided not to return to his room. He didn't want neither company or sympathy. The night was cold and the idea of sleeping exposed on some roof was quickly put out of mind. Passing Barba's wine shop, he remembered the latch key and located it where he had left it that afternoon. He unlocked the door and replaced the key before entering. Afraid a light bulb might attract a passing policeman, he struck a match to find two chairs. He sat in one and rested his legs in the other and leaned his head against a shelf of bottles. It was uncomfortable but he was too sleepy to care.

Tomorrow was already today.

WEDNESDAY

CHAPTER 15

A RATTLE OF METAL ON metal. The sound of wood straining. The blue light of dawn rained across Stephen's face. The day had commenced like a cell accepting its DNA instructions.

"So you are the reason my door is unlocked," said Barba.

Stephen yawned and tried to stretch the stiffness from his shoulders and neck.

"God I'm tired," he said. "You always up this early?"

"Every day of my life. Would you like a Greek coffee?"

"Please."

"How do you like it?"

"Very sweet."

The old man took down his *briki*, the small pot used for brewing one demitasse of coffee at a time. He measured coffee grounds and sugar for one cup, lit a small burner and set the pot on it to boil slowly and build up a good head of foam. Along with his wine Barba was known for his coffee. Islanders would make an outing of coming to his shop as much for a cup of his coffee as to purchase wine and later in the day its' quality would be the topic of conversation at some table.

"I'm sorry I woke you."

"Why, what fault is it of yours that I slept here uninvited?"

Stephen looked out the door at the empty sky. The sun was beginning to yellow the day. He lit a cigarette after offering one to Barba who accepted it but put it behind his ear to smoke with his coffee.

"Sleep is a gift that befalls every man, poor or rich, good or evil. Undisturbed sleep is every man's right."

It's too early for this, thought Stephen.

Barba slammed a piece of cardboard on the table, lifted the carcass of a black beetle and tossed it out into the street. He wiped his fingers on his gray trousers and set the coffee cups and saucers on the table.

"What made you decide to sleep here last night?"

"I've tired of my room and company and it was too cold outside."

"So you came in, good for you."

Barba leaned forward for Stephen to light his cigarette. They sat in silence and sipped their coffees and smoked. A thick residue of grounds settled in the bottom of Stephen's cup. He placed it upside down in the saucer and turned the cup clockwise three times.

"Can you read futures in coffee cups?" he asked Barba.

"No, but my grandmother could and so will my grandson when he has experienced more of life. She predicted it. Some claim that the gift reappears every fourth generation but that may be a superstition."

Stephen's mind was adrift. The jingle of bells drew their attention to the doorway in time to see a shepherd pass by with his flock.

"I love this island," Stephen confessed.

"I was born here. I have lived every day of my life here and I will die and be buried here. I would not exist anywhere else."

Stephen stood up to stretch again.

"Will you see Renas this morning?"

"Most likely."

"Could you tell him I'd like a single room? If I'm not around this afternoon tell him it's alright to move my things. I only have two bags and he knows which they are."

Barba nodded.

"Thank you for the coffee."

"Come back this afternoon for a proper visit."

"If I can."

Stephen stepped into the daylight. The beetle was lying on the hard shell of its back. He kicked it ahead of him as he walked. Unfortunately natural selection applies to species not individuals. He picked up the insect by its leg and tossed it over the cliff side to save his corpse from being crushed. Pigeons on a rooftop cooed.

"*Kýrie eléison.* Rest in Peace."

Sometimes he could feel the sun drying his flesh to dust, imbedding it in the stones.

The courtyard was still. Stephen unlocked the door to his room with the noiseless stealth of a thief. Nancy and Jill were asleep in their beds, Tom in the fourth and Neal on the floor wrapped in a blanket using an assortment of towels for a pillow. Stephen undressed and slipped between the undisturbed sheets of his bed.

Chapter 16

Rest came in unsatisfying snatches. The dehydrating residue of alcohol in his blood stream finally defeated his attempt to sleep and left him cold sober. Jill lay on her side studying him.

"Let's go to the beach and cool off," she whispered. "I want another day exactly like yesterday."

"What's the time?"

"My watch always runs fast," said Jill, consulting it. "When did you get in, I didn't hear you."

"Dawn."

"Did you have an amorous adventure?"

"You'd better wake the others."

"It's still early and they're dead to the world. Let's have a smoke first."

Jill rose from bed wearing only the thigh-long T shirt she slept in. She took out a cigarette from Stephen's pack, lit it and brought it to his bed to sit with him.

"Why's it so beastly hot in the morning?"

"No circulation. Open the door a bit."

"Later," an exhalation of smoke," what did you do till dawn?"

A cloud descended on his mind. Without consciously thinking he began playing with her left nipple. The sensation seemed to entrance her and she watched passively as her nipple tightened and its imprint showed through her shirt. She leaned forward and kissed his eye lids.

"Do you want me to make love to you?"

He turned his head apathetically. The room seemed loud with sleeping breaths. Jill lowered the sheet that separated them. The sleeping breaths grew louder. She straddled his hips and he could feel her wetness. The sleeping breaths grew faint. She slipped him inside her but he could not make himself feel a part of the coupling.

"Stephen, make love to me."

He looked into her blue eyes, eyes that were so beautiful to watch when they lost control; but he could not overcome that moment's air of déjà vu.

"Fuck me. Don't worry about *them*, they don't exist."

"We need an ashtray."

A glass rested on the floor beside Jill's bed half filled with water and the yellow remnants of cigarette butts. She took the cigarette from his fingers and dismounted him. The Germans entered the courtyard laughing and playing a cassette of Beethoven's *Eroica*.

"Bloody hell," she cursed as the cigarette hissed out its life. "They've killed it. Everyone will wake up."

Stephen sat up in bed and pulled on his jeans.

"I may as well wash up," Jill complained, putting on her bikini.

She thrust the door open with a loud crash. Sunlight flooded the room.

"Everybody up," she shrieked and walked into the courtyard.

"Good morning *Fräulein*," one of the Germans greeted her. She ignored him as she passed.

Chapter 17

The café on April 21 Street was open for business. Its proprietor had been released by the authorities and was working diligently to recoup the losses incurred by his day in jail. He was not the kind of man to realize that his labors were an exercise in futility. No tour boat was expected that day and what belongs to a moment in time must be lost when it passes. That is the true meaning of lost.

Stephen and Jill were finishing breakfast by the time the three caught up with them. He had just informed Jill that his plans for the day did not include going to the beach with them. She took the news as a personal rejection and, although she had no rights over his time, was quick to verbalize her disappointment.

"Stephen doesn't want to come to the beach with us," she informed the others as soon as they sat down at the table.

"That so," said Tom, indifferently.

"That so! Apparently our company isn't intriguing enough for him."

"Really Jill," Nancy tried to calm her down.

"You can change your mind," said Neal. "We could get wasted and contemplate the waves."

"Sounds nice but I can't," said Stephen.

"Why not?" Jill hounded him.

"I have things to do."

"For instance?"

"Things that don't concern you."

Stephen was getting angry at Jill for feeling that she had a right to question him and he did not feel like inventing a palatable excuse. Jill remained irritated with him.

"I'll go back for our towels and stop by the grocery. The rest of you can meet me at the bus stop. Bastard," she said to Stephen.

"I'll go with you, I'm not hungry anyway. Are you coming?" Neal asked Tom.

"Nancy and I will meet you. Temperamental little bitch," said Tom while attempting to decipher the menu. "What did you have for breakfast?"

"Coffee and bread and butter with honey," said Stephen.

"Is that okay with you Nancy?"

"If I can substitute tea for coffee."

"Who do I order from?" Tom looked about the room.

"The man next to the old woman behind the counter, but you'd better go to him if you want service in the foreseeable future," said Stephen.

"What do I say?"

"Café au lait and chi and then point to this and this on the menu. He'll get the message."

Tom crossed the room to place his order.

"I hope Jill's tantrum didn't upset you," said Nancy.

"It didn't," said Stephen.

"Good. You have things to do and they're none of her business. She can be difficult at times. Now maybe you can understand what I've had to deal with. She plays men along and when they refuse to submit to her childish whims she turns on them."

"So?"

"I think you should know that she and Neal would have been intimate last night if Tom and I hadn't been in the room."

Stephen wanted to laugh. The universe was on the verge of comic hysteria. There he sat bombarded by people who sifted past him like watery fragments of a dream taking themselves and their relationships with him seriously, even expecting a commensurate degree of seriousness from him.

"Good morning."

It was Esther; wearing the same halter-top, shorts and sandals she had on the night they met her. Physically, she was one of those petite girls with incongruously large breasts. She had just parted with a young man at the door who Stephen glimpsed when she entered.

"I think I got it across," said Tom.

He and Esther sat down together and Nancy introduced them.

"I wish I could have made it yesterday," said Esther. "Did you enjoy the beach?"

"Fine," said Nancy, "we met Tom and his friend Neal. We're going back today if you'd care to join us."

"I have to help Laki reorganize the shop. His father gave him an article that said merchandise should be periodically rearranged to increase sales."

Breakfast was served and wordlessly consumed. Nancy and Tom departed for the beach with an abbreviated, "Bye."

"Guess I should be going too," said Esther, lingering unprepared to leave like a displaced person with no where consequential to go.

Stephen gazed out the café's glass doors into the street.

"Seek and you shall find, ask it shall be given," he said.

"What did you say?" asked Esther.

"Seek and you shall find, ask it shall be given."

"You don't say."

"Do you believe it? Literally I mean."

Conversing in the street with the Trekas boy was the girl Stephen had seen yesterday at the beach and last night at the discotheque.

"Could be true."

"How?" he wondered, keeping a close eye on the girl's movements.

"If it means that a person will get what they want if they want it badly enough."

"So if someone knows what they want they shouldn't be afraid to go all out for it because they're sure to get it?"

"I don't know how sure it is, but if you want something badly enough."

"Can you see that girl in the street?"

"Yes."

"Know her?"

"I've seen her around. She and some friends stopped by Laki's shop the other day but they were leaving as I went in. She's a pretty girl," Esther read his mind.

The girl had concluded her business. She and the boy passed out of view traveling in opposite directions.

"Are you coming or going?" Stephen asked Esther.

"Staying, I've got a sudden craving for a dish of yoghurt."

Stephen was in the street in time to see the boy turn down Rue Marinatos. The girl was gone and though he could probably have located her he wanted to know what they had talked about. He caught up to him.

"The girl you were speaking with, what did she want?" he asked him.

"A horse to ride down the cliff," said the boy. "She is going to the volcano this afternoon."

"How many horses did she want?"

"She said I want one horse."

"Just one," he wanted to be sure. "What time does the boat leave for the volcano?"

"Two o'clock or whenever it is full."

"Could you meet me here at one? I too need a ride."

"Yes."

"Don't be late."

"Of course not," said the boy, slighted at the mere suggestion.

Stephen sat down on the cliff wall. The volcano's barren crater island, Nea Kameni, the New Burnt One, rested benevolent and serene surrounded by the azure sea.

Perfect, he thought. If things don't happen by accident perhaps they happen by design. Who knows where it might lead. That's where I'll meet her.

Not a cloud.

Chapter 18

Three hours to murder. Stephen returned to his room to shower and put on his bathing suit under his jeans. More murder to commit. He located a barber shop and bought a shave and had his moustache trimmed. More murder to commit. He wandered aimlessly through the mayhem of Thira's northern alleys until he found himself at the doorstep of the archaeological museum he had passed the night before. Being its first visitor in several days, the uniformed guard was convinced that he must be a student and allowed him entrance for half the admission fee.

The one storey marble structure was built about a vacant, earthen courtyard and contained visually unimpressive exhibits, but its air conditioning was a cool respite from the heat. There were cabinets of trinkets, few worked in gold, fragments of amphora and, in various corners, large, partially reconstructed urns with geometric patterns. The bulk of the display was wooden pedestals topped with chipped marble busts of classical deities or prominent personages and fragmented torsos of armless, legless, headless figures.

Hunger. He left the victimized remains of long forgotten egos and artistic dreams, bought a loaf of bread, warm from the oven, a baked fish, feta cheese, Kalamata olives, ripe red tomatoes, a lemon and salt and returned to Barba's shop.

"I brought food this time," he told the old man.

"Good. Come in. I have been expecting you. You see?"

A bottle of wine and two glasses had already been set out on the table in the shop's dark heat.

"We need a knife."

"I have one somewhere."

It was in the work bench and Barba wiped it clean on his sleeve. The tomatoes and cheese and lemon were sliced. Stephen sipped some wine and broke the bread, scattering crumbs across the table

"How could you be so sure of my return?"

"How does one explain the unexplainable? I've told Renas you want a private room. He has one and will come by again later this afternoon to take you to see it."

"I'm going to the volcano."

"You will be back by sunset. I'll tell Renas to look for you then." Stephen nodded.

"What about the young ladies you were with yesterday?"

"We're going our separate ways."

"Too bad," Barba poured more wine, "the one was a doll."

Having delivered that sentiment with the solemnity of a postmortem report, he and Stephen turned to the fish. They ate as though the channels to the brain that controlled thought and speech had been switched off, until Barba's grandson stuck his head inside the doorway.

"*Papou*, you told Kyria Vassilliou you'd deliver her a bottle of wine for lunch."

"Eh?"

"Kyria Vassilliou."

"You take it to her."

"I have horses to get ready."

With those words the boy darted off. The old man rose slowly from his chair.

"The Devil," he cursed. "Eat. Drink. I shall return."

When he reached up for the woman's bottle, he came across the manila envelope Stephen had left with him last summer and returned it to him.

"You better take it back before I misplace it. Age plays tricks on a sane man's mind."

During Barba's absence he thumbed through the hand written pages of a half finished poem without removing them from the envelope. By the time Barba returned he was smoking a cigarette and drinking a final glass of wine. The old man sat down at the table again, nibbled a few more bites then pushed the food aside.

"I've lost my appetite," he said. "Business can drive a man crazy."

Stephen offered him a cigarette and lit it. He studied the old man's wrinkles and wondered if the forces that carved those creases had done so with the premeditation of a Michelangelo seeing the final shape of his sculpture within a solid block of marble. Barba held the cigarette upright between his thumb and forefinger and puffed carefully to preserve its lengthening ash intact.

"What troubles you Stephanos? Last year you appeared to take pleasure in life and this year you seem to be drowning in thoughts."

"Circles."

"Circles?"

"Nothing ever changes. Nothing. Not really."

"You dare to say that to an old man who was young not so long ago?"

"That's not how I meant it."

"Then?" the old man smiled at his victory.

"Lately I've begun to feel condemned to relive the same life that others have already lived countless times before. That I am not me or ever will be."

Barba laughed.

"If that's what troubles you then let me assure you that you are you."

Stephen did not like being misunderstood. What point was there to a conversation if he had to constantly stop to explain the process that had led him to a thought?

"There's more to it than that," he said.

"What? Or do you think that I'm too old and feeble-minded, like that Kyrie Thori, to understand? For some age brings wisdom and for others the depressions of a worthless life."

"Freedom."

"It's only a word."

"The only word that I believe in and the only way to avoid reliving another's life. So I tell myself that freedom exists but I don't feel free. I wake up every day feeling imprisoned."

Barba leaned forward in his chair.

"To me it is not so complicated. You are free if you are satisfied and happy and those things come only from God."

"I'm glad it's so easy for you Barba. Something happened to me today."

"Yes, yes, go on, more wine?"

"There's a girl that I feel a great need to meet and I think I have begun to meet her. I am telling you this because for a moment this morning when I saw her I felt free and that disturbed me."

"Why?"

"I don't know."

"Listen to me," said Barba. "You or me or all greatest men that have lived cannot begin to realize or understand the amazing complexities of life. Only God is capable of such knowledge which is why we are children to Him in our ignorance. It is as he planned."

Mortal beings will have their myths, thought Stephen, but did not interrupt.

"Life is a parade. That is all you need to learn and accept. I learned that lesson as a boy. Life is what God makes it. The reason

I have never traveled is because I know that God will allow me to see what he wishes me to see and no more no matter where I am. As for intensity of feeling, that is a gift of Santorini."

There was nothing else to be said. Stephen finished his wine and stood.

"I have to go to the volcano now."

"Let me wrap up the rest of the food for you."

"No, make hors d'oeuvres out of it for your customers."

"Then take some wine," said Barba, "this small bottle."

Not wanting to argue, Stephen accepted the gift and stepped out of the cavernous darkness into the sunlight.

"I will have Renas look for you at five," Barba called out after him.

"Fine. Oh, I left my envelope."

"Never mind, I will have Renas deliver it with your bags if you promise to say hello to the old man for me."

"What old man?"

Barba pointed down the cliff.

"The volcano and aloud so he can hear you."

At the juncture of Rue Marinatos, Stephen sat on the parapet and looked down at the volcano. I won't say a word to her, he thought, until we're out there.

CHAPTER 19

Under the green, sun-bleached canopy of the café at the base of the island, Stephen bided his time. The shaded air was stagnant and the buzz of crickets muffled the lapping murmur of the sea. Swooping out from a hollow in the cliff, a sea eagle swam across the ocean of sky and circled the small neighboring island of Palea Kameni in search of lizards.

The Trekas boy had been on time but, as he expected more riders, Stephen descended the cliff alone. The situation suited him. He wanted to be alone with his plans and expectations, to try to find a reason why he was going to such lengths to meet the girl. It was atypical behavior for him. He generally allowed encounters to happen by chance as they had with Jill, or not.

It was the hottest part of the day and nothing stirred about the dock except the café owner and a neglected dog named Argos. Stephen ordered a Coca Cola and glass of ice from the proprietor and bought a Persian melon to take on his trip. He cleared his mind and shifted his chair to face the crater island in an attempt to draw from it some premonition of his immediate future. Impossible.

Nearing two the launch arrived. Suddenly, it appeared from around a bend in the cliff announcing its presence with a cacophony of chugs. Its two-man crew, commanded by Kapetan Charon, moored the vessel and busied themselves on board with engine maintenance,

Manifesting in lots, the passengers began to arrive. A quartet of two elderly Romanian couples actively engaged in conversation; two South Americans, a rugged aristocratic man about forty with a young man; a pair of Australian men in their twenties paralleled in stride followed by a Greek youth. A time lapse. Finally she arrived, alone, without her friends. In sequence, they paid their passages and boarded the launch. Stephen found himself wedged in at one end of the boat's two benches between the motor and the Greek youth, across from the girl. She took cautious but pleasant notice of him with her eyes before focusing her complete attention to their destination.

The launch set off. Ignoring orders to be seated, the middle-aged South American stood at the prow of the boat with one foot on its rail, poised like a conquistador about to discover an unknown land. The illusion of an irenic sea was dispelled as soon as the launch was free from the cliff. Exposed to every flow of wind, swells of water rocked the wooden hull exploding into drenching particles of spray. Midway between Santorini and the crater island the South American elected to take his seat for fear of slipping overboard.

Twenty minutes into the voyage, Kapetan Charon steered into a sheltered cove that was blanketed with buoyant pumice. Born of lava overflow, Nea Kameni was an arid, black scorched piece of earth that resembled a lunar landscape. The passengers disembarked with the trepidation of astronauts unsure if the loose soil would support their weight. They huddled on the cement quay puzzling over the view and what a volcano looked like and how to recognize it and in what direction to walk to find it. They looked to the Kapetan for guidance.

"*Frurio,*" he said, "volcano, pfft," and he waved his arms in a simulated eruption. He pointed the direction and sent his crewman to lead the expedition.

"You're not coming?" Stephen said to the Kapetan before stepping ashore.

"It need be seen but once," he replied, unbuttoning his shirt. "I come here to bathe. The sea in this cove is warmed by the volcano. Very therapeutic, full of minerals. Sometimes the gasses that seep in change the color of sea to milky white or yellow. But that is usually before it blows up again," he laughed at his joke.

"Seems clear today, you can see the stones on the cove's floor," said Stephen.

"So far today," Kapetan laughed again.

"So far is good enough for me. Can I leave this fruit and wine onboard?"

"No need to ask."

"Help yourself," Stephen offered and hurried to catch up with the others.

CHAPTER 20

It was a hot and difficult hike to the center of the caldera. The compact unit that set forth from the inlet was soon a straggling line strung out across dusty hills of sliding tephra. At times, the tail of the column lost sight of its head. Those with cameras bore them like lead weights about their necks. The girl wore leather sandals that persistently filled with soil. At one point, she balanced herself precariously on one leg to remove a pebble from the sole of her foot, and Stephen grasped hold of her arm to prevent her from sliding down an incline. Her expression was her gratitude. They didn't speak but, as they started up again, he was sure their public relationship had germinated.

The crewman was the only one who maintained a steady pace. Dogging his heels were the Australians. A gaping distance behind them were the South Americans, then the Rumanians making their progress as a collective group, then the girl. Stephen and the youth brought up the tail.

"Have you been to the volcano?" Stephen asked him.

"Every two weeks in the summer," said the youth. "My father sends me to collect rock specimens from the center of the volcano to sell to the tourists. That's why I carry this satchel. My name is Demetrius."

"Stephanos. The Kapetan should have let you lead the way."

"What are you saying? Do you think I want to be responsible for his passengers? One died on him last year of a stroke. See? Look at them."

The Rumanians had stopped walking. The excessive heat and their ages were too great a burden. They let the girl pass by but motioned Stephen aside and asked him to take one of their cameras to the volcano and snap a picture. In their Italian sounding language, dabbing his forehead with a handkerchief, one of men managed to convey that the aperture and exposure were set and all that Stephen had to do was focus the lens and depress the metal knob.

"How much farther Demetrius?"

"It's about forty minutes from the cove."

"What do you get for your rocks?" Stephen asked to take his mind off the monotony of the trek.

"It depends on the size of the rock, its colors and the customer."

More heat. More sweat. More hills.

At last the end was in sight. The crewman and the Australians lingered atop a steep summit and peered down its incline. The South Americans and the girl arrived at the site. As Stephen neared the group he could smell the biting stench of sulfur emitted from the fumaroles.

The goal, a studied purview of the cavity that had decimated the intricate Minoan palaces at the insular pinnacle of their glory, had been achieved; physical evidence of the capricious forces beyond man's control with the amoral power to transform hope for the future into a lethal and senseless past. For some, a phenomenal curio to be photographed, as Stephen did for the Rumanians.

Such were the thoughts the scene evoked; but the girl was there, straight and beautiful and seemed to cradle hope within her. Why not, he had searched everywhere else for it. She had already driven him to lengths. Perhaps it was time to stop allowing external events to play upon him with complete apathy as though he worshipped fate; or because it seemed to him that there was nothing of consequence, one could do to break the repetitious cycles of life that engulfed all creatures. Mankind was bound up in a cog toying at existence, manufacturing elaborate games and rules to follow with a pattern of superficial rewards to while away the time until death.

Whenever he felt himself playing a role, that his identity was false, he rebelled. To what ends? To other roles? If rebellion had ever brought a modicum of satisfaction it was fleeting and hollow;

yet the choices at those intersections had been rebel or be enslaved. So he rebelled; rebelled from people and situations and opportunities that he interpreted as concealed bribes toward conformity. And now, in the blackness of his intellectual despair, the girl was there.

Demetrius began his quest for rocks. The rim had been combed out by tourists and the pickings were paltry.

"Nothing *good* up here," he said to Stephen with a salesman's eye for merchandise. I have to go down there to find quality. Would you help me out again? The crewman doesn't like me and the others are foreigners."

"For the price of a rock."

"Done."

"A *good* one from as close to the center as possible."

Demetrius skidded angularly into the basin unleashing a trail of dust and landslide of stones that rattled like a handful of colliding marbles. Locating a geological treasure trove, he went to work.

"I found yours," he called up to Stephen.

"Toss it to me."

Demetrius' didn't have enough on the throw and the rock was lost on the slope.

"Here, another just as *good*."

Stephen caught the second offering. It was an interestingly fused rock about two inches in length with sharp edges and a colorful blend of yellow and green and red and black. He examined it then walked over to the girl who had keenly watched the procedure.

"For you," he said, placing it in her palm.

She half shook her head in a negative fashion.

"Yes," Stephen insisted, closing her fingers about it. Taken aback by her coolness, he withdrew before she could directly refuse his gift.

Satisfied that the visitors had seen their fill of no man's land, the crewman began the return trek. The group fell into line behind their guide.

"Time to go," Stephen told Demetrius, too absorbed in his work to notice their departure.

"Coming. Nothing to worry about. The Kapetan always waits until about five before returning."

To scramble out of the crater, Demetrius had to sustain a running start that slackened with every step. It was as he reached the top and the ground gave massive way beneath him that he needed to reach for Stephen's outstretched arm.

"You alright?"

"Fine," Demetrius dusted himself off.

"I hope you know the way back, the others are out of view."

"By memory."

Stephen took a final look at the heart of the volcano. Barba says hello he thought. But a sense of guilt overcame him and he paused. The old man had specified that he wanted his greeting to be delivered aloud and, although he felt foolish, he shouted down into the chasm,

"Barba sends his respects."

He waited, almost expecting a reply. Nothing. A loose train of earth trailed down the opposite side of the crater kicking up enough dust to be picked up by a twirl of wind.

Chapter 21

Anchored in the cove beyond the launch was a white yacht. Displayed at its stern were two flags that indicated the ship was registered in Greece and chartered by Australians, taking a winter break from home. Lounging on recliners on the immaculate deck, with tall drinks in their hands, resting away the weariness of rest, was a pair of couples in their fifties. By the ship's gangplank, a uniformed crewman kept a chaperon's eye on two young women who snorkeled close to the hull.

They were not alone in the sea. The two Australians were swimming out to them. The South Americans in shorts had waded out to their knees and the Rumanians investigated the shoreline for sea shells and other keepsakes in ankle deep water. Only the girl remained apart from the people infested cove, at the far end of the quay, cooling her toes in the surf.

One of the Australians swam up to the young women and tried to talk with one of them. The girl's father observed the encounter and carried his drink to the yacht's railing.

"Time for you to come on board Catherine," he called down to her.

"Alright Father," she obeyed, stroking toward the ship with her sister.

"You touring the islands sir?" the swimmer persisted, directing his question up to her father.

"Right you are."

"Going to Crete and Rhodes?"

"Among others."

"Me too. I just stopped off on Santorini to see the volcano, me and a mate. We're from Melbourne. You play bridge?"

"Sometimes," said the man, watching the girls being helped onto the yacht.

"Need a fourth? I have three Master points."

The young women safely out of reach, the man ended the conversation by turning his back on the bather.

"What was that fool yelling his head off about?" the Kapetan asked Stephen, using Demetrius' Swiss army knife to cut the Persian melon Stephen had brought into wedges.

"He wanted to go on board and play cards with them."

"Cards," the Kapetan laughed, "that's a good one. Play with one of those girls would be more like it but Baba said not, eh?"

"Maybe he just wanted a free ride to Crete."

"That one's even better. The idiot should know that the rich never give you anything for free. There, your fruit," said the Kapetan arranging the wedges on a platter.

"Help yourselves," Stephen invited him and Demetrius and the crewman, "and give the rest to whomever wants a piece. How much longer do you plan on staying Kapetan?'

"When would you like to leave?"

"Later, after I finish my fruit."

"Take your time."

Stephen took two slices of melon and the wine onto the quay. He attracted the Rumanians' attention and pointed to where he returned their camera. Done.

The time had come. The others in the cove were occupied. There was no postponing it. If he was going to speak with the girl it had to be then or never.

She was sitting with her back to him, facing Santorini's cliffs. Crossing the quay, he felt nervous and reprimanded himself for it. The world was not about to be created or destroyed.

Meet her with the same equanimity you have when you run into girls like Nancy and Jill, he thought. At last he was there and forced to speak.

"Would you like a piece of melon," he said, kneeling beside her, "and wine?"

"*Merci*," she said and accepted the fruit with an encouraging smile, so he sat down beside her.

"It was a long, hot walk and I thought you might enjoy it."

"*Oui.*"

"You're French," he said and laughed at the way that revelation came out.

"Is that bad?"

"No," he smiled. "Sorry, I didn't mean it in any particular way. It's just that…"

"What?"

"In the time I've known you I never considered the reality of your existence as a person with a personal history."

"But we just met."

"We just spoke, but we've known each for longer."

"How long?" she wiped some juice from her lips with her finger.

"Two days. We met yesterday at the beach and last night at the bar and you've been in my mind ever since. That's why I bought this fruit for you."

"You tease me," she complained. "Why would you have bought this melon for me when you didn't know I would be here today?"

"But I did. Last night I had a dream about it. Did you like the fruit?"

"Very sweet."

He offered her the other wedge and she accepted it.

"And some wine?" he asked

"*Non, merci.*"

He wanted to know more about her but was reluctant to ask too personal questions for fear of alienating her. He drank what wine the Kapetan had left him and watched her eat the melon slice.

"Are you from Paris?" he finally asked.

"Yes, although I was born in Nice. My father's business brought him to Paris when I was very young. Since my grandmother's death we rarely return to the south. I miss it very much. The sea is warm and the people friendly. Have you been to France?"

"To Paris when I was a child. All I remember was the rain and the way people looked like ants from the Eiffel Tower."

"Then you haven't seen Paris. You should go back."

"Perhaps next time you'll be in Paris and you could introduce me to your city."

The girl's eyes became uneasy. She pretended not to have heard what he said as though its dismissal would expunge it from her consciousness. It seemed to him that she was struggling to forget his presence; that her attention no longer belonged to him.

It's no good, he concluded. She's tied to something and I'll remain irrelevant to her. It's that simple.

He was fumbling through his mind to find the phrase that could exorcise the tension when Kapetan Charon called out to him in Greek.

"Are you ready to leave? Kameni is no place for love making. Be kind to the girl. On Santorini we have beds. Warm, soft, intimate beds."

Damn him, Stephen thought, what if she understood Greek?

"The Kapetan is ready to return to Santorini," he told her.

"Yes."

Stephen helped her to her feet.

"Thank you for the melon and the stone," she said with what he interpreted as an air of finality and they walked to the launch.

CHAPTER 22

Stephen sat beside the girl during the return trip but they did not speak. The engine was too loud and the launch was crowded with silent strangers and his optimism had waned. Life was pointless again. The mutual necessity of their meeting might have been a trick of his imagination manifested by the loneliness of despair.

Approaching Santorini in daylight, the cliffs could be seen as arid geological strata of earth, magma rocks, pebbles, basaltic deposits, and ash streaked with gray, white, black and pink pumice.

It was not the solid black wall it appeared at night but the exposed flesh of the island's intestines.

The Trekas boy was the only horse master on the dock when the launch returned. Since Stephen and the French girl were his only clients, the three rode up Rue Marinatos together. The boy trailed the way clicking this tongue to encourage the beasts that moved in spurts, colliding at bends in the course. Atop the cliff, Stephen helped the girl dismount, convinced that opportunity would be his last to touch her. But as they climbed the remaining steps into Thira she asked him if he spoke Greek well enough to help her find the post office. A reprieve? He left her on the corner of April 21 Street to solicit directions then collected her.

"I didn't mean to make you take me there," she apologized while they walked.

"I have time and the directions were confusing."

He spoke the truth. Time only existed to appreciate her and finding the post office was challenging enough to require additional directions along the way. He could think of nothing to say to her as they walked except that she was beautiful but a warning he had memorized some years ago made him refrain: *The wise lover does not praise his beloved until he has won her...the fair, when anyone praises them, are filled with the spirit of pride and vainglory.* All philosophy is open to debate but he saw no reason to put that wisdom to the test.

He stood by the window in the makeshift post office while the girl picked up her mail. On the sill, two flies rested one atop the other while a spider wove its web above them.

"*Non, non, pour* Danielle..." she told the clerk behind the metal bars and printed her surname on a scrap of paper.

The clerk finally located a small package and made her sign for it. Still coupled, the flies absconded.

"*Allons-y*," she said to Stephen, forgetting he was not French. "A birthday present from my mother."

"It's your birthday?"

"Last week."

They walked together toward the center of town with him trying to think of a way to extend their encounter, when Renas found them on March 25 Street. He wanted to show Stephen his new room.

"Thank you for everything," she said to Stephen and before he could stop her she abandoned him to Renas.

"Danielle," he called after her and she stopped walking and turned to face him.

"How do you know my name?"

"From the post office. Mine's Stephen if names matter. Why did you run off?"

"I didn't. I've taken enough of your time and your friend..."

"My landlord has another room for me."

"And I have things to do this afternoon."

"Can I help you with them?"

"No."

"Could I take you to dinner tonight? To celebrate your birthday."

"No. People are expecting me."

"Couldn't you meet them later?"

"They're not in Thira. We are staying at Akrothiri."

"You could call them."

Danielle hesitated as though searching for a way. She'll stay, he thought, if you can make it easy for her.

"No I can't. The last bus for Akrothiri leaves at seven and if I miss it the only way to get there is by taxi and there is only one taxi on the island and..."

"I'll arrange it. Meet me at," it had to be a place where there would be minimal chance of running into Nancy and Jill, "at the

Hotel Atlantis in an hour. If I can't get a taxi there will still be time to catch the bus and if I do I'll have him come to the hotel at nine or ten?"

"Eight. My friends expect me for dinner."

"Eight."

"Yes," she smiled and they parted.

Stephen returned to Renas and good-humoredly put his arm about his shoulder.

"Now where is this room? And before I forget, tell your father I delivered his message."

"Message?"

"To the volcano. And I have a favor to ask. I need a taxi tonight at eight at the Hotel Atlantis. Is that possible?"

"It is my cousin's taxi."

"I didn't know that. Do you think he would be available?"

"He will be there."

"For sure? It's for that girl you saw me speaking with."

"She's with the archaeologists at Akrothiri."

"You know them?"

"No, but I know of them."

Chapter 23

Stephen's new room was on the opposite side of Rue Marinatos from the one he shared with Nancy and Jill. It was built directly upon the cliff rim in a more secluded area. Stephen followed Renas along April 21 Street then down a series of circling steps that passed close by a church and ended by a series of stairs that ascended to an abbreviated walkway. On that level four more stairs, which formed a right angle, mounted to a courtyard streaked with streams of flowing water that cascaded over the terraced dwellings filling their storage tanks.

Two doors faced the courtyard, one violet colored and the other green. Renas told him that behind the violet door lived an ancient woman named Rhea. A recluse of sorts, she rarely ventured from her room except in the predawn hours of days she visited the produce market. Her sole companions were a melodious yellow canary, hatched and reared in captivity, whose bamboo cage she hung out above her lintel each day, and a stray orange and white cat named Nemean that adopted her. How and when she had taken possession of her room Renas was unsure because it had been given to her, free of charge, for the duration of her life by Barba when he was a boy too young to take notice of such things. To the islanders her background was a mystery. She made her living by caring for the room Stephen occupied and hand sewing a few dresses each year sold in one of the tourist shops. Renas assured him that his privacy would not be disturbed by her because she never interfered with the goings on about her. As he and Renas passed through the courtyard, Rhea cracked the door to eye them.

"Good evening," Stephen nodded to her and received a suspicious silence for reply.

"Another lodger," Renas identified Stephen and the door was closed and latched.

Stephen's room had the luxury of a private bath and a small window that overlooked the sea. It was clean and furnished with a dilapidated double bed, a table with lamp and chair and a chest of drawers with a mirror with layers of wood stripped off its frame. Above the bed an icon of Saint Irene, the island's namesake, concealed a break in the plaster. On the wall facing the head of the bed a frayed tapestry had been hung.

"Does this meet with your approval?" Renas asked.

"It's perfect."

"It was the room I held for you in June."

"I'm sorry to have put you to so much trouble."

"Until August I usually have extra rooms," Renas handed him the key. "Could you tell me how much longer the English girls will be keeping their room?"

"You'll have to ask them."

"If you need anything just let me know. Do not be concerned about the old woman. She is bizarre but harmless."

"You won't forget about the taxi?"

"No."

There was an hour before Stephen would see Danielle again, if at all. He wondered if her friends would keep her from him but there was nothing he could do about that. He decided not to think about it for the moment and settled into his new place and took a shower.

Stephen traveled light. He fit the contents of his two bags in one bureau drawer. Unpacking the loose sheets of the second section of his poem, he added them to those in the manila envelope Barba had remembered to send. Toward the bottom of one bag, wrapped in a T-shirt, was his revolver. He left it in the bag and folded and crammed both bags in the bottom drawer.

The water in the tank had been filled in the late afternoon and not warmed by the noonday sun. Stephen's shower was icy cold but shedding his journey's dust and sweat was a pleasure. Dried and dressed, he fell fatigued on his bed. He glanced at his writing but the words and stream-of-conscious images did not interest him.

Outside the window the light of day paled. His eyes were attracted by the interplay of shadows across the tapestry on the wall. Though bleached of most of its color, it retained the lines of an interesting arabesque design. He wondered if its weaver had been artist enough to conceal some esoteric message in its threads. In the four corners were mosques bordered and connected by pressed flowers. Within the square, four cloaked maidens rode galloping white horses, all mirror images. Encircled by the riders was a maze of interlocking vines and in the center a dark ellipse.

Afraid of dozing off, Stephen lit a cigarette.

CHAPTER 24

The dining room of the Hotel Atlantis was cool and clean and empty. Danielle was not there.

Stephen chose a table in the back, farthest from the plate glass window that looked out onto and in from April 21 Street. Privacy. He wanted Danielle alone. Half an hour elapsed. He twice dismissed the jacketed waiter and was about to give up hope of seeing Danielle when she arrived. She stood in the doorway, a shopping bag in hand; her eyes seemed almost frantic until they noticed him and relaxed.

"Is this table okay?" he stood to welcome her. "We have our choice."

That was not precisely the case. The Rumanians from the volcano had occupied one of the remaining ten.

"Yes," she sat beside him and placed her shopping bag in the empty chair next to her. "I've passed this hotel but this is the first time I have been inside."

"Me too."

It was a hospitable room broken up by wooden pillars that supported wicker baskets of hanging vines. In various spaces grew potted, broad-leafed plants and red geraniums.

"I'm glad you came," said Stephen. "I was looking forward to it." "Me also."

"When you were late I worried that, was it difficult for you?"

"No," said Danielle but qualified her response to, "yes and no. I have to be back in Akrothiri by nine."

"I arranged for the taxi to be here at eight."

"Was it difficult?"

"I don't think so. Anyway, I didn't want to risk your clothes turning into rags."

"What do you mean?"

"Do you know the story of Cinderella?"

"Yes, yes," she smiled with understanding," and my taxi will become a vegetable."

"A pumpkin," he said.

"*Citrouile*," Danielle laughed, "is there a more absurd word?"

He watched her lips form the word "absurd" and wanted to kiss them. It was then that he noticed that she was dressed differently from earlier that afternoon.

"Is that a new dress?"

"Yes, isn't it incredible? All handmade by an old woman on lives on Santorini; she makes only a few each year," Danielle stood to show it off.

"And new sandals," he observed, "and painted toe nails."

She blushed at that and took her seat but her eyes reflected the excitement of her purchase.

"I saw it yesterday in a shop but was talked out of buying it. The owner told me about the old woman but not who she is. If people find out who she is she will stop making dresses he said. Feel how delicate, it has the texture of lace."

"You should have let me go with you."

"No, it was something I had to do alone."

Stephen could relate to that.

"Do you like it?" she asked.

A simple white cotton dress with a variety of intricately embroidered blue leaves and trim, it buttoned in the front and fell loosely to her knees. It was similar in fashion to a style of peasant dresses available in most island tourist shops but of a rare artist quality that Danielle recognized and appreciated. She wasn't wearing a bra and the cut of the dress insinuated the perfect roundness of her breasts, modestly concealing the points of her nipples behind embroidery.

"I do, and like you it has a certain *je ne sais quoi*," he said, proud of his choice of words, but almost as though she could read his mind she lowered her eyes.

"Why did you invite me tonight?"

That was a more serious question and he didn't know how to answer it. He lit a cigarette to stall for time and played with it in the ashtray.

"I asked you for the same reason you chose to come," he finally said.

The waiter returned with menus and a pitcher of water and a basket of bread. He set everything down and withdrew to give them time to decide on their order.

"Are you hungry?"

"I shouldn't have come. My friends are waiting to have dinner with me."

"And you can't disappoint them."

"I saw you with your friends yesterday," she reminded him, "you understand."

"They weren't friends but I do understand," Stephen thought it wise not to pressure her. "The taxi won't be here for another hour and meantime we could drink some wine to celebrate your birthday. That would be alright wouldn't it? No one would have to know, we could keep it *entre nous*."

She smiled and offered him her hand to seal the bargain. Stephen ordered a bottle of champagne from the waiter and *tarama*, a fish roe paste to go with the wine.

"Have you done a lot of traveling?" he asked to make neutral conversation.

"To Spain and Italy and Scandinavia with my family and Greece last year, but this is my first time to Santorini."

"Did you learn any Greek?"

"*Un peu.*"

"Enough to find the post office?"

"No," she smiled, "that would be difficult."

The waiter arrived with the wine and *tarama* and uncorked the champagne and poured two flutes. Stephen lifted his glass to click Danielle's.

"*A votre santé,*" he said, "and happy birthday."

"*Yassou,*" she replied in Greek with a calculated smile.

"Alright, next time I'll toast you in Kanarese then what will you say?"

"*Prost,*" she laughed and Stephen laughed with her.

Whatever Stephen imagined he had seen in Danielle's eyes yesterday at the beach he felt confirmed. Somehow, her presence had the power to bring him peace. Though he tried not to be obvious, he could not avoid staring at her, at her eyes, her lips, at her slender fingers that would be a sculptor's dream. He broke off a small piece of bread and put some *tarama* on it and offered it to her. She opened her mouth and he placed it on her tongue.

"What brought you to Greece?"

"I study painting and art history at the Sorbonne. One of my professors brought a group of us, who will do postgraduate work, to Greece to study the art firsthand. We stayed in Athens mostly, the museums you know, but took trips to Mycenae and the Peloponnesus and Delphi and Crete."

"The grand tour."

"I want to be an artist and just paint but I come from a very practical family who feel it is important to study something that can lead to a living, like law, like my sister. My aunt was a ballerina when she was young and convinced my father that art history offered a number of possibilities and studying it has helped me with my painting."

"You like ancient art."

"Especially pre-classical. Some find Cycladic figures and Minoan frescos primitive but they are mistaken. Picasso understood. When figures are disproportionate or if compositions lack depth or seem too geometrical I think it says more about the society of the time than the artist's skill. Artists sculpt and paint the way they see life. People never truly understand artists."

"Do artists ever understand themselves?"

"If they live long enough. Often they die too young."

"Is that why you're here on Santorini, to study art?"

He fed her another bite and topped her wine glass again.

"Yes and no," she said, becoming pensive. "I am here with a friend, an archaeologist and his professor and a colleague who are here to study the Minoan site at Akrothiri. Professor Gossard wanted an artist along who could make accurate sketches and Andre proposed me and... We have rooms at the hotel built at Akrothiri that accommodates visiting archaeologist."

"You and Andre," he said without meaning to.

"All of us and the professor and his wife. But tell me something about yourself," she said to change the focus of the conversation.

"What for example?"

"You're an American but do you live in Greece?"

"Yes, in Athens but for how much longer and why I can't say. My life is changing and in turn changing me."

"How?"

"This is no place to discuss such matters. There's a café at the end of the street, we could have a coffee..."

"The time," Danielle said, consulting her watch. "And you would not want to take me there."

"Why not?"

"Yesterday morning my friends and I had some difficulty there. The police came and took the owner away. All over a misunderstanding, but Andre and the owner were easily angered."

Stephen recalled the café's bolted doors. It was strange to consider that their paths had crossed even before he knew of her existence.

"Then tomorrow, we could meet in the plaza and go to the beach," he said.

"I can't come to Thira tomorrow."

"There's another beach at Akrothiri. I don't know the name of it but it has a beach of pebbles. Do you know it?"

She nodded.

"We can meet there tomorrow at noon."

"Impossible."

The conversation had reached its inevitable climax. From then on, Stephen knew that his words would determine whether he would see her again. He decided to go for broke.

"Nothing is impossible," he said. "You are a person who has the right to decide how to spend your day. After all, once it's spent it's lost forever."

"No, there are my friends and my work."

"Your friends are archaeologists; let them go about their business while you go for a swim. They don't expect you to sit beside them all day long with a sketch book in your lap do they? You don't have to mention me."

Danielle shook her head.

"I saw you yesterday at the beach, last night at the discotheque. Not once did you laugh. Tonight you're happy weren't you?"

She nodded almost reluctantly.

"I was happy too and that has become a rare experience. What harm is there in two people who make each other smile going for an afternoon swim?"

Danielle was quiet. There was nothing else to say. It entered his mind that if she turned him down nothing prevented him from going to Akrothiri on his own initiative, but he would not do that.

It had to be her decision. Before he could elicit one, the waiter came to the table to tell him the taxi had arrived.

"I can't be sure," she said at last, standing and collecting her shopping bag.

"I'll be at the beach tomorrow," he said. "Come if you can. Can I keep you company on the ride back to Akrothiri?"

"No, that would not be a good idea."

Stephen saw Danielle to the taxi. He took the driver aside and paid the fare and tipped him to be sure he saw her safely in her hotel. He turned to Danielle and they parted without any show of affection.

Chapter 25

10:02.

"Want some company?"

Stephen had finished the remainder of the champagne and tried not to think about the attention Danielle and her dress and sandals and polished toe nails would receive in Akrothiri. He ordered a plate of *marithes*, fried fish, and a Fix beer and tried to convince himself that hope, even if it is an illusion, existed for the moment and that the moment was best left at that. He had settled his bill and the busboy had cleared the dishes and he sat arranging formations of bread crumbs on the table cloth while he summoned the will to go home.

"Am I disturbing you?"

Stephen looked up at Esther. She seemed lonely for companionship.

"I don't think so," he said.

"But you're not sure?"

"Sit down."

Esther complied.

"I see you managed to meet her," she said about Danielle. "Does this mean you can find if you seek? Who is she?"

"An artist with the archaeologists at Akrothiri," he dusted away the bread crumbs and leaned forward on the table. "Would you like something?"

"Nope. And if I did it would be better to order for myself. They'd just tack it to your bill. The man at that table talking with the waiter is Laki's father. He owns the hotel."

"Oh," Stephen lethargically absorbed Esther's announcement.

"Having a boyfriend whose father owns a hotel has advantages like free food." A pause. "I ran into your friends this afternoon. They were looking for you."

"That so?"

"Jill said if I saw you before she did to tell you she apologizes. I don't know what she meant by that but I guess you do."

"No idea."

"Damn it!"

Stephen straightened up. "What's the matter?"

"That…" Esther swallowed her expletive.

Stephen turned to find the source of her aggravation. Two tables away were the South Americans from the boat. They were the only diners left in the room and the middle-aged one was lifting his wine glass to Esther.

"Bring your friend and visit with us," he said to Esther.

"Damn," she repeated in a subdued tone.

"What's the problem?" asked Stephen. "So he likes you, take it as a compliment and dismiss it. No need to get upset."

"It's not that easy. He's been hounding me since he and his friend rented a room here. Do you know how bad that looks to your boyfriend's father?"

"No," Stephen admitted, sizing him up. "What do you say, shall we join them? I could use the distraction. You can blame it on me later."

"I don't know."

"Let's go," Stephen decided for her.

Together they crossed to the South American's table. He stood to guide Esther into the chair beside him and shook hands with Stephen but didn't bother to introduce his companion.

"Don Aliveros."

"Stephen."

"Thank you for gracing my table," he said to Esther.

"I only came because Stephen wanted some distraction," she told him point blank.

"Then I redirect my gratitude to you," he said to save face. "I remember you from the boat this afternoon. Would you like a glass of wine?"

Stephen shook his head and lit a cigarette.

"Esther please come here," Laki's father ordered her in Greek.

She excused herself from the table.

"You will return to us?" said Don Aliveros.

"Maybe."

An embarrassing silence. Stephen regretted his decision to visit Don Aliveros' table. There was nothing he wished to say to the man, nor was he interested in learning anything about him. His plan had been for Esther to bear the burden of conversation in the hope that its trivialities would help him stop obsessing over if Danielle would meet him tomorrow. But instead of returning to the table, Laki's father led Esther out of the dining room. Stephen had decided to just get up and leave when Don Aliveros asked where he was from.

"America."

"*Los Estados Unidos*," he said to his companion who made a face at the information.

"What's his problem?" asked Stephen.

"You're a citizen of the United States are you not?"

"I just told you so," Stephen was irritated.

"No, you said you were American and only a person from the United States feels that America is synonymous with his country. Do not be offended but we Argentines are not fond of the United States for political and economic reasons."

"That's hardly an original view within or without the United States."

"But my convictions are of a more personal and intellectual nature."

Pompous ass, Stephen thought.

"I should explain that I am committed to a universal cause that cannot tolerate the tyranny of capitalist nations."

"What's that?" Stephen looked around for Esther.

"The cause of social justice and equality and the revolution that must bring these things into being."

"For the good of mankind or the good of Don Aliveros?"

Don Aliveros was insulted that his integrity was questioned.

"I am a rich man," he raised his voice, "yet I am not a capitalist. I could be, and a most successful one, and oppress the poor."

"So how did you become rich?"

"That is irrelevant. What is relevant is that for the last decade I have worked to advance these principals in my country."

"Then why aren't you home working for the cause?"

"A man must learn in order to be helpful and traveling is an educational experience."

"Are there a lot of you? To spread the word I mean."

"I have a number of disciples."

"You see yourself as a messianic figure?"

Don Aliveros smiled.

"How much does anyone know about Christ and the origin of his mission? And if he was among us today in another body how would we recognize him? How would he recognize himself? He had doubts about who he was during his first incarnation."

Stephen shook his head.

"Ah, here she is our Esther come back to us at last." Don Aliveros said. "Sit down, sit down."

"I only came to say goodnight," she said, looking at Stephen to communicate that was his opportunity to escape.

"But why?"

"I'm sleepy and I've got to meet Laki."

"I'll go part way with you," Stephen seized his opportunity to stand.

"But our conversation, we have barely scratched the surface. My concept has many complexities that should be explained."

"Another time," Stephen said devoid of such intentions.

Esther and Stephen moved before another overture could be made. They did not even reply to Don Aliveros companion who had finally condescended to open his mouth and bid them, "*Buenas noches.*"

"If I'd known before going over there that you were going to desert me…" Stephen said to Esther when they were out of earshot.

"I couldn't help it," she said. "It wasn't my fault and I tried to warn you."

"I'm not sure if he was serious or putting me on."

"Dead serious. Incredible isn't it?"

"What?" Stephen asked as they reached the door. "*That the best lack all conviction while the worst are full of passionate intensity?*"

"That while some people struggle to hold themselves together with glue and string, others sit idly by drawing up grand schemes to rule the human race."

"Is something the matter?"

"No, nothing is ever the matter. Goodnight Stephen."

Chapter 26

April 21 Street. Cloudless sky. Cool night air.

The lights of Kyrie Thori's taverna were being extinguished. On its roof, a perched owl hooted.

Walking in the starlight in the empty street he heard the sound of familiar voices tracking him. Looking over his shoulder, he made out the shadowy figures of four people that his mind's eye identified as Nancy and Jill with Tom and Neal. His first instinct was to avoid them and an explanation of why he had tired of their company. He was physically drained from the long trek to the volcano in the heat of the day and emotionally spent from his dealings with Danielle. As the voices neared, he looked for an alley to dissolve into and found he was stranded by the cliff wall. Clinging to the dark, he was considering the drastic measure of hanging over the cliff wall to remain undetected when the quartet passed him by: two couples but the Germans who had been his neighbors.

He arrived at his room annoyed by his irrational behavior. Undressing in the lamplight, he noticed that the extended hooves of the tapestry's galloping four horses had been repeated by its weaver in its corners like reflections in a pond. He lit a cigarette and lay back on his bed to study the tapestry but all his mind envisioned was Danielle.

She stood before him in her white dress and he undid her buttons and slipped his hands inside about her waist and drew her close and kissed her open mouth and inhaled the scent of her. He closed his eyes and was asleep while today was still today.

THURSDAY

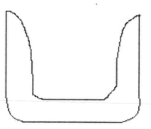

CHAPTER 27

THUS SPOKE THE CANARY: "CHEE chee che che che chee che che cheeeeeeeeeee che che chee che che cheeeeeeeeeee che chee che..."

Stephen sat up in bed. Daylight through the window sunned the floor of the room. He lit a cigarette to sober his yawns and begin the great struggle to regain possession of his life from sleep.

You're on the island of Santorini, he thought himself conscious. At this moment there are insects warring, birds soaring, elephants sunning...dolphins mating. There are people being destroyed for reasons they can't understand or don't even exist. Today you will go to the beach of stones and Danielle will be there or she will not. If she is you will begin something with her or you will not. What a seer you'd make.

With those words he urged himself out of bed and to the shower. He wore his swimsuit under his jeans, grabbed his towel and hurried out past the canary trilling hopelessly for a mate.

CHAPTER 28

Stephen crossed April 21 Street and went directly to the plaza in the back of the town. He had breakfast in the same café he had patronized with Nancy and Jill the day they went to Kamari beach. He waited for the same bus but for the route it ran at an earlier time. There was comfort in that fact. It had been his experience that tourists tend to discover few secrets about the places they pass through and rarely take buses to unknown destinations, especially when they know a beach that has been tried and true. Also, a ship was scheduled to pass Santorini at noon and his old roommates might have decided to be on it.

There was time for a second cup of coffee. He crossed the room to place his order with the proprietor who was kibitzing two old men's animated game of *tavli*, backgammon. On the way back to his table, he found a discarded copy of yesterday's *International Herald Tribune* and checked the sports page to learn the Red Sox had won on homers by Yastrzemski and Petrocelli.

The bus to Akrothiri was half full and Stephen sat up front near the driver and watched the lean landscape flow past. The route paralleled the cliff until it reached a fork in the road that cut inland. At that juncture the driver announced "Akrothiri" over the public address system. It was then it occurred to Stephen that if Danielle intended to keep their rendezvous she should be at that stop. She wasn't. Only a light-complexioned, black-haired Greek girl on the verge of womanhood boarded the bus. She was intriguing to look at with facial features that replicated those of the procession of Minoan woman from the fresco at Knossos an ancient artist had captured for posterity.

"Where is Akrothiri?" Stephen took his eyes off her to ask the driver.

"There," he pointed across a field of fledgling grape vines.

"I see nothing but dirt."

"It's where the land slopes down to the sea. It is the last point your eyes can distinguish. You have seen it but you can't make it out. It is both there and not there," the driver smiled through his decaying teeth.

"The beach we're going to…"

"The next stop."

"Could someone staying in Akrothiri get to the beach from there?"

"There's a path along the shore. But hotel guest usually go to the small cove on the other side to swim."

By mutual consent, the conversation died. It was a gusty day and the clouds of dust that sporadically pelted the windshield absorbed the driver's attention.

CHAPTER 29

The beach spread out beyond a row of trees that bordered a farm-er's furrowed field. To one side, a taverna with a covered patio faced the sea. In the immediate surf, two young Spanish women cavorted topless in the waves while a third, in a one-piece suit, encouraged their frolic. As the bus passengers dispersed like bands of primates to stake their territories, Stephen checked the patio for Danielle. Not a trace. He looked for her along the shore. Just beyond the point where the number of bathers thinned out, he heard his name and looked up toward the trees and saw her. When he reached her, she kissed him on both cheeks, as if greet-ing a friend.

"What made you pick up here?" he asked.

"It's more private and the beach is full of stones"

"I might not have found you."

"You would have," she smiled.

Stephen spread his towel beside hers.

"We have an odd relationship," he said. "We plan meetings but until I see you I'm never sure you're going to be there."

"It is the same for me. I didn't know if you would come. But it is best this way. Because we never know if we will meet again we must be happy if we do. It makes our relationship unique. Shall we test the water?"

The beach was on the southern part of the island unsheltered from the wind that stirred the waves and wore the stones to a pol-ished smoothness. It brought the currents that made the sea too cold for Danielle and too turbulent for an enjoyable swim. They sat at the shore's edge.

"Do you ever try to judge how far a wave will push the sea?" she said, playing with a handful of pebbles.

"Sometimes. That one will touch your toes."

"No, it will be swallowed by the one behind it and neither will reach me. You see? I win the bet."

"We didn't bet anything."

"Then you can owe me a wish."

"That's not fair."

"I know. It is a game I play with myself to cheat life."

"What does it get you?"

"Oh, a wish I don't deserve."

"Do any come true?"

"If a wish came true it would no longer be a wish."

"I'll take your word for that."

Danielle laughed at the look Stephen gave her.

"My grandmother loved the beach," she said. "Cold water never bothered her."

"This was your grandmother from Nice?"

"Yes," she said, as they walked up to the tree line to escape the glare and heat off the stones and the wind. "When I was a young girl I would stay with her in August while my parents traveled and every day she would take me to the beach. I played in the soft sand and she gossiped with her friends. Before going home she would carry me into the sea and splash water until I was wet all over and ran crying from the waves. She would wrap me in a large towel and rub me warm saying 'Danielle cold water is good for your blood.' When I was dry she did like this with her fingers on my stomach and I would laugh until I could not cry."

They had reached the narrow stretch of red sand beyond the stones where Danielle had spread her towel. She took off her kaftan and folded it to use as a pillow. Like the Spanish girls at the other end of the beach, she only wore the bottom piece of her bikini, not uncommon among European women so Stephen did not read anything into it. She lay on her back and used her hand to shield her eyes from the rays of sunlight through the branches and watched Stephen undress.

"Have you been in Greece long?"

"Some time," he said.

"What have you been doing?"

"Waiting."

"For what?"

"You perhaps."

"You like to tease."

"No."

He knelt beside her. They studied each others' faces in silence until he leaned to kiss her and she closed her eyes and parted her lips and their mouths touched. The kiss lasted for several minutes and became passionate then exploratory then almost too light to feel then intense again until, like coupling, it was suddenly spent. To regain herself, Danielle took a deep breath and slowly opened her eyes. The passion of their first kiss confused them. Stephen straightened up, without allowing their bodies to touch, unsure how to react. He looked at her feet and ankles, then the flat of her belly, then her breast, then her mouth, then her eyes to see if they reflected what she felt. She smiled and reached out to touch his cheek.

"I can't," she said and reclosed her eyes and turned her head aside.

CHAPTER 30

Danielle watched Stephen walk out of the sea and up the beach to her.

"Did you enjoy your swim?" she asked.

"Too rough to swim."

"Is the water cold?"

"Feel for yourself."

He lay down beside her and she ran her hand across his chest and stomach.

"How long did I sleep?"

"Half an hour or so."

"I'm sorry. I didn't mean to. I closed my eyes and..."

"Did you enjoy it?"

"It was so peaceful, like a dream without being a dream."

"Then you shouldn't be sorry. Besides, it gave me a chance to think."

"About me?" she smiled.

"Mostly."

"And the rest?"

"What you asked me before, what I was waiting for. I said you but you didn't seem to want to believe that. I understand, after all we're complete strangers, unless we've never been strangers at all."

"What do you mean?"

"I live a life of desperation. When I look back over my life it seems as though I have always been desperate, for no particular reason I can put my finger on, and the years only make it more intense. Just to justify living has reached the point of being illogical."

"I understand that feeling."

"Of course, because you had to."

"Why do you say I had to?"

"This is what I reasoned while you were sleeping. You can tell me if I'm wrong. The first conscious relief from desperation I can remember was when I saw you at Kamari. I can tell you the exact moment; it was when my eyes saw yours and understood that at the same time your eyes were seeing mine. Seeing not just looking at.

And the desperation reflected in each other's eyes was momentarily cancelled. Our eyes understood that, which is why I said perhaps we've never been strangers."

"It's an interesting thought."

"Are you content with your life?"

She didn't answer.

"Right now, here on this beach?"

"Yes."

"Later tonight with your friends?"

Danielle did not reply.

"Why do you become quiet when I mention your friends?"

She shook her head.

"Come back to Thira with me. We can spend the evening together and get to know each other."

"No."

"I'm not trying to trick you into bed if that's what worries you."

"No."

"Look, I don't understand it and I can't explain it any better. I only know that I saw you and the universe realigned. And it's not as if I ever believed in love."

"I can't because Andre and I are engaged. I'm sorry, I should have told you."

"And that's why you bought that white dress and new sandals and..."

"No, buying the dress was for me but I wore it for you."

"But you went home to him."

"It's not like that between us, not like..."

"Our kiss."

Danielle blushed.

"How long have you been engaged?"

"He'd been proposing for the last year." She was sitting with her legs folded, clutching them with her arms and lowered her forehead onto her knees. "I accepted him the morning before you saw me at the beach."

"Camus was right, the world is absurd. Do you love him?"

"Why do you need to know so many answers?"

"Because I haven't the luxury of time. I don't know when you're leaving Santorini and I'll never see you again. If you want I'll follow you to Paris, or you can stay in Greece with me."

"No more Stephen."

"I'm sorry."

CHAPTER 31

They dressed and went to the taverna for cold drinks. They sat on the patio and looked out on the beach and barely exchanged a dozen words. The intimacy that had developed between them was strengthened by their silence. Stephen knew that Danielle was trying to tell him something and he waited for her.

"I'm not in love with Andre."

Those words came out of her like a confession from the depths of her soul. They seemed a revelation and confusion to her.

"The kiss made me understand. But Andre loves me. I know that. And I love him. What do you want from me?"

"You," he said.

"What does that mean? It is important that I know."

"I'm not talking about desire, although there is that. I've become too cynical to believe in salvation but if there's such a thing I'm sure you can only find it in another person. I'm also sure that if that's true it can only come once. For us it might be each other. At least we should find out."

"What about responsibilities to other people?"

"We're talking about the difference between living and just existing."

"Yes, but I know other things too. After my grandmother died we moved to Paris. It was there that my parents and Andre's became closer than friends. They are inseparable. We're supposed to meet them in Tuscany on our way back to Paris and I thought, oh I don't know what I thought. Andre and I are their only children. We were raised together and it is the fulfillment of our parent's lives that we marry."

"And you accept that?"

"It has been a truth of my life."

"And you accept that?" he repeated. "And Andre too?"

She gave the impression she didn't want to talk about that anymore and became silent.

"I must get back," she said at last.

"I'll walk you."

"No, I can ride the bus. It leaves you closer to Akrothiri than walking back from here."

They spent the remainder of their time strolling along the shore stopping at intervals to touch and kiss, having acquired the sensual affectations of new found lovers. They had discovered a tenuous security in each other's presence. At last, they returned to the farmer's field to await the bus.

Chapter 32

They sat in the rear of the bus as far as possible from others. They sensed their desires and the futility. Circumstances could not have been better aligned against them. It was as though the fates had woven the pattern of their meeting in order to laugh at them.

"Come tonight," he said. "If you need a reason, tell your friends it's to meet the old woman who made your dress."

"But that can't be and what if one of them wants to come with me."

"It's just a reason. I'll wait for you in the taverna on April 21 Street down from the Hotel Atlantis."

"If I'm not there by eight…"

"Akrothiri," the driver announced.

Danielle kissed him once more and worked her way to the door. Stephen relinquished his seat to catch a last glimpse of her, soon obscured by the cloud of dust raised by the bus tires.

You'll never see her again, he thought. But what did you expect to come of it? Think. You're no better than a madman drifting through a sea of humanity without direction. Is that the kind of lure with which to entice a lover, especially one with a preplanned life?

The feeling of emptiness had returned.

Thira town was waking from its afternoon slumber. Streets and alleys were filled with the sounds of unbolting shutters, plants being watered, mothers calling children and dogs barking.

Stephen returned to his room to shower off the sea salt and sweat. He failed to notice that Kyria Rhea had made up his bed with the meticulous care of a person with only one mundane chore in life. If he had, he might have checked to make sure his gun had not been disturbed. Instead, he flung open his window to let in fresh air. Inevitably, his eyes contacted the arabesque tapestry that was the sole spot in his room that was not an eyesore. His gaze transfixed on the center of the design and he became mesmerized. The faded colors seemed to brighten to liquidity and the four maidens on horseback began to race round it in accelerating circles. They started a train of thought.

Subtlety is the essence of reality, life. What is obvious is of no importance. The only thing of value is what is implied. Subtlety lifts us to a plane above our ordinary state. It's in the air above our heads, just beyond reach. There, everything must make one total sense. All that occurs here means something else there. Like the beach this afternoon. Like the way every word meant touch me, save me, prove to me that there is a point to life. There must be a way for every human being to break through the barrier. I know *there* exists because poetry comes from there and I have experienced poetry. Danielle.

Stephen broke the tapestry's spell and dismissed his notion. His environment was intolerable, his room was a prison. He dressed and went to café in the plaza for *ouzo*. As the proprietor delivered his drink, his old roommates entered the establishment.

Chapter 33

"Speaking of the devil," Jill drew their attention to Stephen.

Each greeted him but they sat at a table nearer the doorway where a breeze could be felt. Only Jill came to sit with him.

"I apologize for having called you a bastard, you wanker," she said.

"We are all bastards and bitches," he replied.

"I knew you understood but that demented little witch over there has been throwing the incident in my face ever since."

"You're not alone in here," Nancy reminded Jill.

"Demented, eavesdropping little bitch," Jill amplified her comment.

"I don't need this," said Stephen.

"Sorry," Jill lowered her voice. "Have you missed me?"

"I've been preoccupied."

"I've missed you."

"You've had company."

"Is that what you think of me?"

"You know that's not what I meant."

"I'm young and I act as I want. I don't intend to become perverted like Nancy because of regrets."

"What the hell are you talking about?"

"Stephen wants to know what kind of perverted person you are Nancy, shall I tell him?"

"I have enough faith in Stephen to know he'd never believe your dribble," said Nancy.

"Can I have a sip?" Jill pointed to Stephen's *ouzo*.

He nodded.

"Mmm, I love the taste of liquorish," Jill reset the glass. "Since you deserted us our concierge charged Tom and Neal rent."

"It's only fair if they're living there."

"But he wouldn't have if you hadn't left. I'm trying to make you feel guilty. Where are you staying now?"

"In another room."

"Yes, but where?"

"If I drew you a detailed map you wouldn't be able to find it."

"If you showed me I could come by for a visit later tonight."

"I'm busy."

"Neal and I are going, you coming with us?" Nancy asked Jill.

"She dragged us to a monastery today," Jill complained.

"Atop Mount Profitis Ilias, the highest point on Santorini; it's worth the trip for the view," Nancy defended herself in parting.

"We saw two of the old boys sitting under a fig tree in the court-yard," said Jill after Nancy and Neal had left. "Why do monks and nuns look so perverse?"

"Perverse seems to be your word for the day."

"Seriously. They look positively sinister. It's because they live unnatural lives."

"You don't have to be a virgin to join."

"But once you do you're supposed to remain chaste and that's unnatural."

"They believe that abstinence is an aesthetic experience that brings them closer to God,"

"Aren't they the fools?"

"What if it brings them contentment?"

"Contentment! I read that an early Christian saint, as a young man, had himself castrated in the name of Christ. At the end of his life he wrote that he didn't feel it had been necessary. Not necessary to never make love. Oooooh," she shivered.

"This subject really seems to interest you."

"Oooooh," Jill shivered again. "Will you have dinner with us tonight?"

"I can't."

"How much longer will you be staying on Santorini?"

"I don't know."

"Promise you won't leave without saying good-bye. Even if you don't like me."

"I don't dislike you and I promise."

"I'd better go take my shower before our water tank runs dry again," Jill stood up. "Coming Tom?"

"I'll meet you at the taverna."

Jill was gone.

"Mind if I join you?" Tom asked Stephen.

"Stay there, I'll join you."

Stephen picked up a Coke from the proprietor behind the counter on the way.

"Just find a place to make your stand and take it easy," Tom recited. "I believe that."

"There's no difficulty with taking it easy, it's finding a place to take your stand that's the hassle," said Stephen.

"I guess," Tom agreed, "unless anywhere suits you. I've missed having you around. What've you been up to?"

"Nothing in particular. I came to Santorini to get away from people and..."

"Understood, you don't have to explain to me."

"Good," Stephen liked Tom for that.

"I heard Jill ask, are you having dinner with us? We'll be at the same restaurant you took us to. The lesbian refuses to eat at the other taverna because of some old guy that got her drunk."

"Nancy's not a lesbian."

"Didn't Jill tell you about…"

Before Tom could finish his sentence Ether rushed into the café.

"I've been looking everywhere for you," she said to Stephen. "You've got to come with me."

"What are you talking about?"

"Kyrie Thori's gone mad. Out of control. I'll tell you on the way."

"Want me to come along?" asked Tom.

"No, I doubt it's anything," Stephen dismissed the emergency.

"You sure?"

"Positive."

"Come on," Esther tugged his arm, "before he hurts someone or himself."

CHAPTER 34

"He's been drinking nonstop since yesterday," said Esther.

"What do you expect me to do about it?" Stephen asked.

"Iphigenia said he's been asking for you."

They entered the taverna to the sound of shattering glass. Thori had thrown a chair at one of the display cases.

"Friend," he said when he saw Stephen then swayed in an attempt destroy the next case.

The door to the back dining area and kitchen opened and Iphigenia looked into the room.

"Do what you can with him, please, before the police come," she said to Stephen and then retreated behind the door when Thori threatened to throw a glass at her.

"Police can do nothing to a free man," he shouted back at her and staggered up to Stephen and embraced him like a long lost son and whispered in his ear, "What is this unbearable misery we call life?"

"Let's sit down."

"Yes," Thori agreed, "and you will drink *tsipouro* with me. Esther, bring us *mezethes* and three glasses, if I haven't broken them all," he laughed. "You know *tsipouro?*"

A form of Greek moonshine, it is made from the pomace of red grapes and more potent than ninety proof *ouzo*.

"A friend on Chios sends me six bottles a year and I have one left. Tonight we will finish it and see where it leads us."

Thori managed to walk to a shelf behind the counter to collect his bottle of *tsipouro*. In the time it took him to complete this task, Esther returned with the glasses and bread and plate of cold octopus and Kasseri cheese and olives.

"Ordinarily I would not allow a woman to sit at a table where I am about to discuss intimate things with a friend but this girl is special," Thori said to Stephen and then leaned forward to kiss her cheek. "Very special, even though there are animals on the dung heap who do not appreciate her. To hell with them all, even your Laki," he said to Esther. "Drink."

They drank to humor Thori. The hope was the liquor would pacify him into a stupor.

"Can I speak to you, friend? Truly speak to you?"

Stephen nodded and offered him a cigarette before lighting one for himself.

"For two days an owl has perched on the taverna's roof." Thori thrust forward two fingers. "Do you know what that means my little foreigner?"

Esther shook her head.

"To the superstitious fools who are my neighbors it is an omen of death," he laughed. "A witless bird chooses my roof because of the mice and they think that Thori must die."

Thori refilled the glasses before continuing.

"Death comes to all creatures for no good reason. And how it is feared. They should fear senility and the decrepitude of age not death. No villager has entered this taverna in two days. The busboy's mother won't let him come to work until the bird departs or I die. My daughter and son-in-law come looking for my corpse. The Devil take them!"

Thori pounded his fist and the noise startled Esther into sitting back from the table.

"I will wait out that nonsensical bird and walk out of here a live man. To death," he turned his head sharply and spat on the floor.

"You're not going to die," Esther tried to calm him.

"Of course I am. I am dead already. We are all dead. We are born dead. Only by being unborn can one avoid death. Drink with me, tonight I can't bear the burden of drinking alone."

Esther could not follow the conversation in Greek verbatim but she understood the gist of it and drank at appropriate intervals.

"She is a good girl," Thori said. "Last night I slept at this table and woke in the dark. I heard the church bell ring and looked in the direction of the sound. Do you know what I saw?"

Stephen shook his head.

"A body was being carried from the church to the graveyard. Inside the church incense burned and the priest chanted. Outside villagers gathered, not dressed for mourning but to observe. The body was mine and the people were waiting to see if my cousin Barba would come to pay his final respects."

Barba and Thori are cousins, thought Stephen.

"I saw Barba coming. He walked like someone who had lost a cherished member of his family. Inside the pious one was laughing.

Everyone was laughing here," Thori stabbed his chest with his finger to signify within. "You were there too but not standing with them or laughing."

"Was I there?" Esther asked.

"No child," Thori crossed his eyebrows. "I don't know where you were. No matter," he shrugged it off, "this is the good part. Barba joined the group. All of them held their tongues waiting for his words of wisdom. My coffin was carried past and he said, 'See what befalls a man who has lost the faith of God.' While they crossed themselves, a murder of crows fell like arrows from the sky and they dug their talons into their skulls. Oooh how they shook and squirmed," Thori aped their writhing, "but the birds would not let go. The streets became red with blood and loud with screams but the crows dug their talons deeper until their brains oozed out and they collapsed on the ground."

Thori clapped his hands and laughed. He poured himself another glass of *tsipouro* but tried to drink it between bouts of sustained laughter and choked and stood up coughing. Stephen and Esther tried to help him but he pushed them aside and made his way to another table. He signaled to bring the bottle and they joined him. He put his arm about Stephen's shoulder and drew his ear close.

"You don't think I'm mad do you?"

"What is madness?" Stephen replied.

"Good, very good," Thori laughed. "It would be unfortunate for you if you did. You would be wrong and you would be a fool."

Thori took a deep swallow of *tsipouro* and passed the bottle to Stephen. His expression turned somber and intense.

"I once had an insight," he said, as though making a confession of supreme importance. "For that gift I have been damned. Look at my existence, my useless leg," he tugged at his pant leg. "I am being punished."

Santorini (A Novel)

"Why?"

"For cowardice."

"I don't believe it."

"I am here. Do you see?"

Either he's drunk or I am, Stephen thought.

"No you do not see," said the old man.

Stephen could not help laughing. He tried to stifle himself for fear of inciting another tantrum but instead Thori laughed with him. He wanted Stephen to drink another swallow.

"Eventually we will reach the same level," Thori said.

Stephen was finding it difficult to shake off a sense of the ridiculous.

"I am not mad, right?" Thori asked again.

Stephen wiped his eyes that had begun to tear.

"Then I must be sane," Thori slapped Stephen's back. "So what have I been doing the last two days?"

"Waiting out an owl?"

That comment amused Thori.

"Are there not more worthless ways to waste one's time? I shall explain reality."

"Slowly," Stephen drank his draught.

"People try not to think," Thori said. "They avoid questions about the meaning of their lives and try to forget them. They delude themselves. They try to escape by keeping their lives in order. Any disturbance confuses and upsets them. So I make noise, like Socrates, and am despised and ridiculed for it."

Stephen wasn't paying attention. He had glanced at his watch and saw it was after seven and remembered Danielle and the kiss and wondered if she would come and if she would be alone and what she would make of the goings on in the taverna and how he would handle things.

"Time is evil," Thori mumbled. "It is both long and short and so can confuse a mind to uselessness. But it all began in clarity. I was born here and played away my childhood with Barba and Rhea."

"Rhea?" the mention of her name caught Stephen's attention but Thori was too self-absorbed to answer.

"I never expected to leave Santorini. I would have grown like Barba with nothing to express but God, God, God. But I had an insight. And my insight told me that a meaning to life could be found if I had the courage to go and seek it. I told my parents good-bye and left."

Thori grew morose.

"I never saw them again. I traveled, I walked, I worked on ships. I surrendered to the flow of life." He livened up. "I lived with whores, stole food, learned the pleasure of perverse women, of opium, of exposure to heat and cold, of the taste of a cockroach."

Thori drank more *tsipouro*. Stephen looked at his bloodshot eyes and wondered that he was still able to lift the bottle.

"Don't you think you've had enough?" said Esther. "I could make you a Greek coffee."

"For thirty years I lived in harmony with the flow of life until the day I learned a tragic truth; that we are all fragile creatures," Thori snapped his fingers in Stephen's face, "that close to becoming the barbarians that we are behind the mask of civilization. That day I killed a man because that was where the flow of life had led me. That was the day I lost the courage to go on and decided to return and married and..."

Thori's hands began to tremble. He used the one to steady the other.

"But I found it, the meaning, I..."

Before he could be helped, his body convulsed and he collapsed on the floor.

CHAPTER 35

Esther helped Stephen turn Thori over on his back. His breathing seemed steady.

"Get his daughter," Stephen said.

Esther hurried into the back room and returned with Iphigenia. Her hair disheveled, her apron stained with sauces, she timidly approached her father's body.

"Is he dead?" she asked Stephen.

"No but you should get the doctor. He may have just passed out but he had a convulsion and I don't know what that might mean."

"Too much to drink," said Iphigenia.

"Maybe not."

"Too much *tsipouro*," she insisted. "I won't call the doctor. My father refuses to have anything to do with him."

"In his condition he wouldn't know," said Esther.

"I can't risk that. If he found out I would fear for my life."

"Don't be ridiculous."

"You don't know him as I do."

"Well you can't just leave him on the floor," Esther shamed her.

"The way he has treated me and my mother he deserves no better, but I'll have my husband come take him home."

"And hurry up."

Iphigenia turned and walked slowly to the door.

"You're sure he's alive?" she asked again.

"Yes damn it," Esther assured her. "Do you think there's something seriously wrong with him?"

Stephen shrugged his shoulders.

"I hope not. He's always been very kind to me."

"It's probably just too much liquor," he consoled her.

"Have you ever seen Iphigenia's husband?"

"No."

"He's no Hercules. I wonder how she expects him to carry Kyrie Thori home?"

The old man moaned. It sounded as though he would regain consciousness but it was a false alarm. He was still prostrate and motionless when Iphigenia returned with her husband, a man in his thirties, about ten years older than his wife. Without mincing words he said to Stephen,

"Help me carry him outside. I brought a mule."

Thori was a heavy man and it was a concerted struggle lifting him off the ground. Esther offered a hand maneuvering the body out the door and straddling it over the mule.

"I can't carry him into the house alone," his son-in-law pointed out, without directly asking Stephen for further assistance.

It was going on eight o'clock.

"I can go too if you need me," Esther offered.

"No, but you could do me a favor," said Stephen.

"Ask."

"I'm hoping to meet someone here at eight. The girl you saw me with at the Atlantis last night."

"I remember."

"I'm worried she might get here while I'm gone."

"I'll wait for her. What should I tell her?"

"That I'll be right back."

Iphigenia's husband took control of the animal's reins and began to walk. Stephen followed alongside the mule with a hand on the body to prevent it from sliding off.

Chapter 36

Thori lived in a section of the town unfamiliar to Stephen so he had to concentrate to memorize the return path. Too dark to make out landmarks, it was like being absorbed in a maze. Dragging the tired beast along, Iphigenia's husband maintained an uncommunicative silence.

Their destination was a cubical, two-storey house encircled by a low wall and a bare, treeless garden. The mule was led through the compound up to the verandah where Stephen waited for Thori's son-in-law to unlock the front door and light the interior.

Thori came out of his stupor while they were easing him off the animal. He mumbled some words about not wanting to leave the taverna before the owl departed, about how such an act could be fatal. But at least he was able to stand and that facilitated the burden of getting him into the house.

The first room they entered was crowded with furniture, worn carpets and assorted bric-a-brac. The walls were covered with icons and other religious paraphernalia. Most of the furnishings contained some degree of red in them, which made a stark contrast to Thori's room just beyond it. Its walls were white, the marble floor bare and dusty and the solitary piece of furniture was an unmade bed beside an open window.

They laid Thori in his bed, oblivious to his environs. His son-in-law removed his shoes and dropped them on the floor. As Stephen turned to leave, the old man caught hold of his wrist and jerked him down.

"Come back to see me tomorrow," he whispered. "If I am not in the taverna come here."

Thori's son-in-law switched off the ceiling light.

"Give me your word," Thori sounded frantic. "I'm not senseless; I know what I say. Don't let anything or anyone keep you away."

"I will return."

"Come and I will tell you the meaning of life. I am not crazy."

Thori released him. Passing out of the bedroom, his son-in-law eyed him suspiciously.

"What did the old man say to you?" he asked. "If he has any valuables hidden here about they belong to his family."

Stephen left without answering him. The evening's events had saddened him enough; a family hating itself and an ailing old man still defying the world and its insistence on conformity. Fortunately, he had to concentrate on finding his way back to April 21 Street and that prevented depression from gaining control. He decided to dismiss the affair by making light of it.

So Thori knows the meaning of life and he's willing to share that knowledge with you. How 'bout that. He knows what mankind has been struggling to discover since the days of Australopithecus. You should look him up tomorrow just to see if he remembers tonight. Could be he's uncovered a Minoan treasure trove.

I'll have to tell Danielle about this, he thought, as though optimism could bring a situation into being.

CHAPTER 37

From the end of April 21 Street, Stephen could see a female figure pacing in front of the taverna. Assuming it was Danielle, anxious about his tardiness, he quickened his pace. It wasn't her.

"She hasn't come," said Esther.

"What happened to the lights?"

"Iphigenia closed up that room. It's a mess."

"She might have gone in the side entrance to the back room."

"I kept an eye on that door too but I tell you she hasn't come."

Stephen refused to take her word. He turned the corner of the building and looked into the rear dining area. There were only two customers, the Australians who shared the launch to the volcano and they remembered Danielle but had not seen her. Esther was still waiting for Stephen when he returned.

"She might have been held up. Why don't we sit on the cliff wall where we can see both doors? I managed to salvage this," Esther held up the bottle of *tsipouro.*

"You don't have to wait."

"I don't mind."

"When, if she gets here we'll have to split."

"I know."

They walked to the wall and sat down.

"Did you get Kyrie Thori home alright?"

"Yes. His son-in-law's an asshole."

"He is," Esther agreed. "Have some *tsipouro?*"

"No."

"She'll be along any minute. Drink some and think of something else and time will fly."

"You have any suggestions?"

They sat quietly for some time, Stephen with his eyes glued to the taverna anticipating Danielle's momentary arrival. When he finally became resigned to the reality that she was not coming, he lit a cigarette to read his watch. It was past nine.

"Join the club," Esther re-imposed her presence.

"What club is that?"

"The stood up for the night club."

"I thought you had a boyfriend."

"That's who I'm referring to. But it isn't his fault. It's his friends."

Stephen was paying little attention to her.

"They say misery loves company," she said.

"So I've heard."

"I don't want to be alone," Esther blurted out. "I'm sorry, I shouldn't have said that."

"Never apologize for the truth."

"It's just the way I feel tonight. It comes over me from time to time. It's a feeling like a cold shiver and it scares me. That's when

I'm literally terrified to be by myself. But it will pass, it always does, it's just for the moment. If you could just sit with me a while longer."

He didn't want to.

"Please," she said.

"I'm hungry, what about you?" he asked.

"No, but I'll keep you company."

"I don't want to eat in a taverna."

"There's the *souvlaki* stand in the plaza."

"It's got to be closed by now."

"No harm in checking." Esther picked up the bottle of *tsipouro*.

CHAPTER 38

Esther's hunch paid off; the stand was still open and the coals of the grill still burning, even though the proprietor was closing up. Stephen ordered several *souvlakis* while Esther claimed two of the sidewalk chairs. The aroma of sizzling lamb doused with lemon and oregano made him uncomfortably aware of his hunger.

"I ordered a skewer for you," he said to Esther and handed her one of two Coke bottles.

"Thank you for the soda but you'll have to eat my *souvlaki*. I'm a vegetarian."

Esther's mind was across the square where some people were walking. They were not identifiable because of the darkness and, before they stepped into another arc of light, they laughed and turned down one of the alleys in direction of the discotheque.

"Do you have to eat your *souvlakis* here?" she asked, without looking at him.

The question was more an urgent request. The tone of it caused him to take conscious notice of Esther. Not in terms of physical appearance that every time he had seen her she might have been wearing the same halter-top and cut off jeans. She seemed to have a deep capacity for pain. What did he know? She might be as happy as anyone can expect.

"Ready," the owner of stand called out.

Stephen paid him and received several bamboo skewers of lamb with a slice of bread spitted on the top of each.

"Where do you want to go?" he asked her.

"Just follow me."

They walked up March 25 Street to where it joined Rue Marinatos. Stephen managed to eat one of the *souvlakis* while they walked.

"Now where?"

"Down there," she pointed.

"Forget it. I'm not walking all the way down the cliff just to turn around and climb back."

"Not to the bottom," she said, starting her descent. "I'll show you."

A third of the way down, Esther located the spot she sought and sat down cross-legged on the low wall that bordered the route.

"Why here?" Stephen sat beside her.

"Because it is half way between the last light and the next one, which attract the moths, and because of what can be seen."

From where they sat, they had an unobstructed view of the dark sea and lighted dock and ship that had disgorged passengers. It had been a dry day and the rain clouds had blown past without surrendering a drop and the mist that usually clung about the cliff had not yet clouded.

"Above or lower than here and you're infested with insects and bats and have to stare at the back of a bush. I'm an expert. I've made a long study of Rue Marinatos. Did you know that the road is named after the archaeologist who discovered the site at Akrothiri?"

"Yes," Stephen began his last *souvlaki* and wished he'd bought a cold beer.

"Whenever I want to be alone at night I come here. You can't be seen from up top."

Esther had a point. There was solitariness about the spot.

"We won't be alone tonight," she said after the haunting baritone of the ship's horn reverberated across the face of the cliff. "We've got the front row seat to the parade of new arrivals."

It was hard to get comfortable sitting on the cliff wall. Esther sat cross-legged with her back propped against the decline of the previous level for support and handed him the *tsipouro*. He took a deep swallow and became aware of the introspective high of that liquor and that he had been feeling it for some time without being aware of it. He took another sip to maintain the buzz and handed her the bottle and lay down on the wall and used Esther's lap as a pillow.

"You mind?" he asked her.

"No, that's fine."

She stroked his forehead, almost instinctively, for something to do. He lit a cigarette and followed the smoke's rise to the stars that seemed particularly distant and endless and thought about Danielle.

The din of hooves and voices reached them. Three donkeys appeared bearing two middle-aged women and their baggage. Walking behind them, a young man with a stick instilled the animals with enough incentive to carry them to the top. He, on the other hand, sat down on the wall across from Esther.

"How are you on this night of nights?" he asked her in Greek.

"Well enough," Esther seemed to know him.

"Where's Laki?"

"He doesn't keep me informed of his every move," she answered without concealing her annoyance at the question,

"Nor do you of yours. Who is your friend?"

"None of your business. You better tend to your riders."

"The animals know the way and I have already been paid," the young man grinned and jiggled some change in his pocket. "What's your friend's name?"

"Stephanos," Stephen replied, "If there is anything else you want to know ask me."

"Are you Greek?"

"A Turk," he answered sarcastically.

"I hate Turks for what they did to Greece."

"So do I."

"Your friend thinks he's clever. From what he said, he hates himself."

"I do hate myself," said Stephen. "So much that sometimes I explode in rage and attack others in the hope they will destroy me and give me peace before I kill them."

Unsure what to make of Stephen, he eyed him warily until one of his customers cried out from above and he ran after the donkeys.

"Why are you hurrying? The donkeys know the way and you have already been paid," Esther shouted after him. "I hope the bastard falls and breaks his neck."

"Who is he?" asked Stephen.

"A spy."

"Who does he spy on?"

"Me. Last October when I arrived from Canada I met Laki and moved in with him. It was natural. Ever since, his friends have been trying to break us up. I can't understand it. In the beginning I thought his father liked me. It all changed when Laki told him we were considering marriage. He's never stated his objections to my face, not in so many words. I don't know what he has against me. If he'd tell me…maybe it's because I'm not Greek."

"Could be as specific as not being from Santorini. Life on the islands hasn't changed in a hundred years. Foreigners come and go but the people remain. They have their own world and ideas about how their children should live their lives."

"I understand that, that's one reason I left Canada."

"And you think that guy was spying on you?"

The next train of new arrivals interrupted Esther. It was Trekas' son and two couples. She took a swallow of *tsipouro* while they passed and offered Stephen one.

"I know it," Esther answered, "he and different people."

"You should tell them all to go to hell," said Stephen.

"It's not so easy. When Laki and I are together everything is fine. But his friends keep interfering. This afternoon two of them stopped by the shop. They met three Swedish girls and invited them to the discotheque tonight. You know how Greek men like blonds. They needed a third to even out the group so they talked Laki into joining them. Not that he wanted to but... then they'll spend the night badmouthing me. Compare me to the other girls and what he's missing. Tell him who I've been seen with, what I was doing at such and such a time. His father encourages them. I don't know how much longer I can stand the situation."

We all have the right to tolerate our lives if we wish, Stephen thought. He stood to begin the walk back up to Thira. He wanted to separate from Esther before he said something that might hurt her feelings.

"Where are you going?" she asked.

"Home."

"Take me with you."

"Home to bed," Stephen emphasized bed.

"I give a great blow job. It's my one exceptional sexual talent."

"Cut it out."

Esther stepped in front of him. "Please take me with you. I can't be alone tonight. Can you understand that?"

"Yes," Stephen understood. "You can stay the night and you're not obligated to provide head."

He didn't know what was going on with Esther and he was in no condition to think about it. But the thought crossed his mind as they walked, sometimes leaning against each other to steady their steps, that it was possible that Danielle had come and that Esther had sent her away. No, that's the *tsipouro* talking, he decided.

CHAPTER 39

Stephen unlocked the door to his room and let Esther enter.

"Home, such as it," he waved his arm and waited for her next move.

He went into the bathroom to splash some cold water on his face. During the walk, he decided to give Esther the chance to reconsider spending the night and leave him to get some sleep. When he reentered the room she was standing by the bed.

"How do you want me?" she asked with the matter-of-factness of a prostitute.

Esther set the *tsipouro* bottle on the nightstand and began to undress. She folded her clothes as she removed them and set them neatly on the floor. When she finished, she turned off the light and crawled into bed. Stephen finished undressing in the dark and joined her.

"This is how it should be when people, you know," she reached out to him, "dark."

Stephen did not find Esther unattractive but she had never aroused desire in him. Perhaps to block out the thought of what Danielle might be doing in bed in Akrothiri or because Esther seemed to require intimacy, he lay down with her. Her breasts were larger than he suspected and he kissed and caressed them in the hope their novelty would kindle an interest in her. They worked their charms but could not transport him to the level where thought gives way to passion.

She kissed the lower part of his abdomen and took him in her mouth and rested her nipples against his thighs and proved the truth about her one talent. Not wanting to be swallowed, he pulled her mouth off him and rolled her on her back. He lay on top of her and she maneuvered him inside her and locked her legs about him and pushed against him. Each time he tried to kiss her, she turned her lips away.

"No kissing" she said. "Slap me." When he didn't she bit his shoulder and said again, "Slap me. I want to be slapped. Slap me, please."

He slapped.

"Again," she said. "Harder."

He slapped her a second time.

"With the back of your hand."

The third time she responded in orgasm and unlocked her legs and slipped him out of her before he had come and pressed him down on her belly and stroked him with her hand until he did and massaged his sperm on her belly and breast as it was a salve.

"Could I have some *tsipouro?*" she said.

They each took a sip and finished the bottle.

"Do you want to take a shower?" he asked.

"No," she said and nestled her head on his shoulder.

They drifted off to sleep. When Stephen opened his eyes, he could see Esther dressing quietly in the dark. He wanted to say something to her but no words were available. She left without speaking.

Enough, he thought, enough of everything. Tomorrow he would go to Akrothiri and get Danielle.

FRIDAY

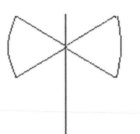

Chapter 40

Why shouldn't he?

Stephen hurried up to Thira on nervous energy. He had analyzed the situation last night after Esther had left. Options had been weighed and balanced like a mathematical equation that lent itself to only one solution. There were no alternatives. There was only one way to go that day and that was to Danielle. Now his mind was preoccupied with finding transport to Akrothiri before daylight made him pause and reflect on the contradictions of night light's logic.

Danielle might have been kept from seeing him or she might have come to the taverna while he was carrying Thori home and Esther might have sent her away. After all, what did he know about Esther and the complexities that motivated her and the degree to which her compulsions might drive her? And there was Danielle's confession that she did not love her fiancé. He might not love her either. If confronted by Stephen, he might remove himself as an obstacle. In the darkness of night his reasoning had made sense.

In the town's plaza he found one of the island's two taxis. Its driver was napping behind the steering wheel with a handkerchief draped over his face.

"Are you free?" Stephen asked him.

The driver lifted one corner of the handkerchief to see who was addressing him. He recognized Stephen and sat up with a broad grin.

"Demetrius."

"Get in. Where do you want to go?"

"Akrothiri."

Before setting out, Stephen bought a warm loaf of bread and two Coca Colas for breakfast. He sat in the front seat with Demetrius and handed him one of the bottles and half the loaf.

"So taxi driving is another one of your talents."

"I don't even have a license," Demetius enjoyed informing him. "This is my brother's cab but sometimes, when he has other business, I substitute for him. After gas, he lets me keep what I make."

They turned onto the road leading out of town.

"How did you make out with your rocks?"

"Already I have to go back to the volcano. Next time I will take two satchels."

Demetrius drove with the strained concentration of an inexperienced driver. Stephen tried to enjoy the ride but the intermittent proximity of the cliff edge and the road kept him tense. Demetrius turned right onto the dirt road that was the last leg of journey.

"Can we avoid driving right into Akrothiri?"

Demetrius pointed to the small settlement ahead of them.

"A path bears down to the left just before we reach there," he said. "That is where you are going. There is nothing down there but a hotel and the ruins. You can walk the rest of the way."

"I will need a ride back but I don't know when."

"Take your time, however long. I will wait for you as you waited for me at the volcano. My uncle lives in that house. Those are his grapevines. I will have lunch with him and my aunt and visit my beautiful cousin."

"Long black hair about seventeen."

"You know Eleni?"

"I saw her on the bus yesterday, if that was her."

"Had to be. She's not really my cousin. She's my aunt's daughter from her first marriage. I'll park the car over there where you can see it. When you are ready to go back," he played a few notes on the horn, "and I will hear you."

Stephen got out at the juncture. He lit a cigarette and began his walk.

CHAPTER 41

Round the first bend, the smell of the sea was in the air and a fiberglass Quonset hut could be seen. A barbed wire fence had been strung about it and by the gate was a guardhouse. It was the archaeological site. Stephen decided to check it for Danielle before continuing down the path to the hotel.

The guard was a congenial Greek with red hair and well-trimmed beard. He admitted Stephen and insisted on officiating as a tour guide. As they entered the hut, he offered some preliminary remarks about the ancient city. Professor Marinatos had personally told him it would take more than a hundred years to unearth it from its lava tomb.

The refracted sunlight through the semi-translucent roofing monochromed the interior sundry hues of orange. The atmosphere was stifling and scented with dust, and the musky odor of decomposed life.

Archaeologists suspected that the city was quite large. Only time and patient scientific study would determine its relative status among other Minoan cities. Perhaps it was the greatest of them all.

"Perhaps the jewel of jewels," said the guard, fascinated like a gem collector beholding a flawless emerald. "I've read what scholars have said about these people and, in my mind's eye, can see them as they were." He looked down one of the excavated streets as if it was a teeming bazaar bustling with tan loin clothed merchants and bare-breasted women in long dresses. "I think it is a blessing," he said, crossing himself three times.

The streets were labyrinthine but not as narrow as they seemed. At several building foundations he identified where there might have been windows and balconies. No Linear A scripts had been found but painted frescos were, in amazing preservation. He was there the day the first one had been discovered and recalled weeping at the sight of it.

They arrived at a control pit where three men and a woman were taking measurements.

"Archaeologists from Paris," the guide explained.

"How many are there?"

"Five."

"I saw only four."

"The other one is an artist. She only comes when there are drawings to be made."

They had made the full circle back to the door of the hut. Returning to the fresh air, Stephen experienced the exhilaration of Odysseus escaping cavernous Hades to the light of day.

The hotel faced the sea and would be next in his search for Danielle. On the ground floor were four rooms the management let. Stephen knocked at each of their doors but received no response and went upstairs to the air conditioned dining room. It was cool and sunny in there. The owner was closing the sliding glass doors that led out to the spacious verandah when he saw Stephen.

"Can I help you sir?" he asked.

"A cold glass of water."

"Come to the bar."

In actuality, the bar was a storage counter. He poured a glass.

"More?"

"No thank you."

"You have been to the archaeological remains," the owner deduced. "It is suffocating in there."

"Yes."

"How did you find them?"

"In need of repair."

The owner laughed at the comment.

"You have a nice hotel," Stephen complimented him.

"I do my best. God willing I will prosper. Someday, many tourists will come to Akrothiri. By then the hotel will be twice this size and I will import sand for the beach. Right now, most of my business is with the archaeologists. Five are staying with us at the moment but they will go back to Paris and another group will arrive next week."

"I saw four of them in the hut. Is the fifth one ill?"

"Swimming," the owner rinsed out Stephen's glass.

"I don't see anyone at the beach," Stephen said looking down at the sea.

"Up a ways," the owner directed with his arm, "the stones are smaller. The bend of the land and the boulder obstruct the view. You should go for a swim before returning to town."

"I think I will."

"Tell your friends about this hotel. They can come to see the excavations and swim and have something to eat even if they are not staying here."

"I will tell my friends in Athens. Thank you for the water."

"Thank you sir."

Chapter 42

The beach in front of the hotel was covered with sharp, jagged rocks. One side of it was hemmed in by a cliff that isolated the direction Danielle would have taken. At the sea's edge, encircled by water each time rippling waves frothed over the rocks, was a large boulder. From atop it, Stephen might have been able to spot Danielle but there was no reason to climb it because he knew she would be up shore.

The rocks made the beach difficult to walk on. It was easier to move along the base of the cliff on firm earth. That was not the same cliff that faced the volcano. In the vicinity of Akrothiri, the land inclined gently to the sea. Parallel to the cove, a cliff had been hewn mostly by sea erosion.

Tracing the natural wall's protrusions and indentions, the view of the shore became localized. Where the beach flattened into a surface of smooth stones, Stephen saw Danielle. She lay unclothed and golden-tanned on a white towel with one arm folded under her head and one leg folded up and the palm of her other hand resting on her inner thigh and she maintained her pose with such absolute relaxation that she seemed statuesque. Her eyes were closed to the sun as if lost in the sublime serenity of a dream and he desired her.

On the beach yesterday he had wanted her but his thoughts were more of idealized love than sex. Now that had changed. Desire for her completely possessed him. It was irrational, beyond seeing a woman and being intrigued by her. He wanted to grab Danielle by her hair and bite her breast and hold her mouth to his and take her and punish her for how she was able to make him feel. He understood how Theseus, upon seeing young Helen, had to have her at that moment or his life would not have been worth living.

Stephen was about to step out of the cliff's shadow and into the sunlight when he heard a voice call out "Danielle!" He saw a young man atop the boulder, hands cupped about his mouth like a megaphone, and backed out of sight. Danielle was equally startled and moved out of his line of vision to put on her bikini bottom and kaftan.

"Danielle."

She did not answer him. Moments later she passed in sight of Stephen, by the water's edge, but he made no attempt to communicate with her. She might have spotted him in spite of his silence, for she lingered by the sea line and tilted her head up and to the left where he stood and in line with her peripheral vision. But she did not turn her eyes to his and if she noticed him she chose instead to respond to,

"Danielle, *vite*."

"*Venue!*"

Not wishing to overtake Danielle on his return walk, Stephen decided to have a swim. He undressed on the spot Danielle had lain and entered the sea. The cool sea washed away the heat and cleared his mind.

Returning past the hotel, Stephen saw Danielle seated at a table in the dining room with the archaeologists. Somehow, she was able to see him too and went to stand by the window he would pass beneath. Her fiancé followed her and when Stephen looked up at them he placed his arm about Danielle's shoulder.

The dominant male in a baboon troop illustrates his status by pretending to mount the females in his group in public view of the other males, Stephen remembered having read somewhere.

CHAPTER 43

Demetrius motioned Stephen to wait for him by the taxi. He was standing near an artesian well with several children. One of them held something in her hand that the others helped place into a small hole. The object was covered with earth and a pile of stones. Demetrius said some words to them and they knelt beside the mound and crossed themselves before running off to play.

"It is a very serious matter," Demetrius confided to Stephen, as he strip-shifted the car into gear.

"What is?"

"The burial of a sparrow."

"Is that what you were doing, playing priest?"

"Yes," Demetrius took pride in his harmless sacrilege. "I did it for the little girl. When she saw the sparrow my cousin found she started crying."

"I didn't see your cousin," said Stephen.

"Not Eleni, the boy, my aunt and uncle's son. I told you Eleni's my aunt's daughter from her first marriage. She's inside cooking with my aunt. She's the most beautiful girl on Santorini, maybe in all of Greece. In two years every man on the island will be her suitor."

"You too?"

"Only if she will move to Athens with me after we're married. I don't want to live and die on Santorini."

"How did your cousin find the bird?"

"Walking by the cliff," Demetius shook his head. "I will not be surprised to learn one day that he has killed himself. My uncle has often punished him for wandering too close to the edge. The earth can give way so easily and he could break his neck. But the boy has his own will," Demetrius laughed. "He told me a secret."

Demetrius' laugh was infectious and caused Stephen to laugh with him.

"What?"

"You must realize that my cousin is a boy learning what being a boy means," Demetrius spoke like a man of the world. "The reason he was near the cliff today is because a woman from the hotel sometimes goes to the beach alone and takes off all her clothes and lays in the sun. Even the danger of falling cannot keep him from going back each day to see if Aphrodite is there."

And if tonight in the quiet darkness of his room his manhood arrives it will come to the image of Danielle, Stephen thought.

"Who knows if he's telling the truth or making it up to keep me from telling my uncle he was at the cliff edge again. He is such a storyteller. If it is the truth, it is just as well he learn about foreign girls. How was your visit to Akrothiri?"

"Not what I expected."

"It is that kind of day."

"What kind of day is that?" Stephen yawned.

149

"One of death and dying."

"That sparrow put you in some mood."

"Not just the sparrow. A man in the town who owns one of the tavernas…"

"Kyrie Thori, I know all about the owl on his roof," the heat made Stephen drowsy. "I helped carry him home last night."

"Then you haven't heard?"

"What?" Stephen straightened up.

"I saw his son-in-law in town this morning buying fruit and bread for the vigilants and he told me the old man is dying."

Stephen slapped the dashboard and startled his driver.

"What's the matter?"

"I promised him last night that I would visit him today."

"Maybe it's not too late."

"I carried him home in the dark. I doubt I could find his house."

"I can show you a shortcut."

CHAPTER 44

Demetrius dropped Stephen behind the square in the back of the town. There were no buildings beyond that point and by walking in a straight line through open fields he would arrive at Thori's house. It stood alone, surrounded by the wall Stephen felt sure to recognize.

He passed through groves of olive and fig and pomegranate trees that were so still only the sound of cicadas disturbed the illusion of a petrified forest. By the time he reached Thori's compound his shirt was soaked and sweat from his forehead stung his eyes.

He scaled the back wall into Thori's yard. Walking round to the front of the house he could hear the muffled sound of lamentations. Seated on the verandah was a silent group of old men, some fanning themselves with their hats. They kept a mournful eye on some squatting children who played a subdued game of marbles in the dirt by the gate.

As Stephen climbed the porch steps, Thori's son-in-law came out the front door with a tray of water glasses. He set it on a table where all could help themselves.

"How is Thori?" one of the old men asked him.

A lowered brow kept with the solemnity of the gathering.

"Can I see him?" Stephen asked.

He seemed to consider turning down the request but instead motioned him to follow him into the house. The living room was filled with mostly old women in black dresses whose heads, despite the heat, were concealed in black shawls. While Thori's son-in-law consulted with red-eyed Iphigenia, who sat apart by her father's door, they studied Stephen and whispered among themselves. Stephen was about to go back outdoors for a breath of air when the doctor came out of the dying man's room. A balding man, he knelt by Iphigenia and clasped her hand and spoke softly to her. A precipitation of tears flowed down her cheeks while she nodded a response. When he completed his piece, he surrendered her hand to her husband and addressed Stephen.

"You want to see Thori, eh?"

Stephen felt an intruder's discomfort as the whispers ceased and all eyes concentrated on him.

"Why?"

Why? Stephen had not anticipated such a question. He considered replying why not but answered,

"He asked me last night to visit him today."

"Did he know then he was dying?"

"How would I know?" Stephen said and thought to himself, stupid.

"He has been rambling about a friend, are you that friend?"

"I might be. Doctor, if it is inadvisable."

"At this point he is beyond advisable. You can see him but even if he is able to speak he may not be coherent."

Stephen followed the doctor into the sick man's room.

"A friend is here to see you," the doctor said to Thori and to Stephen, "go close to him, he is partially paralyzed."

The body beneath the white sheet was not the Thori he knew. It was the limp, pale flesh of a being whose life seemed to be evaporating through the pores of his skin, becoming a part of the unbearable heat. His complexion was almost gray and his face so hollow-cheeked he seemed to have lost half his weight overnight.

The room reeked of dying. Not of the moldy odor of decayed death like the Akrothiri site but a sharper, more putrid stench; a blend of medicines and the smell of a body that had lost its self-control.

Stephen felt sick to his stomach. He had to force himself to approach the bed, which was so low to the ground it was hardly a bed in the conventional sense. Thori acknowledged his presence with his eyes. Stephen knelt beside him, taking up his hand when the invalid made a feeble attempt to raise his arm.

"Friend," Thori's lips showed the trace of a smile.

"I have your *tsipouro*. When are we going to get together and finish it?"

"You will have to finish it alone. See what it all comes down to in the end." Thori spoke with a rasp in his throat that impaired the clarity of his diction. "Still, I think it is better to be a dead lion than a live dog."

Thori's eyelids closed, he was breathing regularly and seemed to have drifted into sleep. He was about to release the old man's hand when his fist clenched. Turning to Stephen, he moved his lips in emulation of speech. The sound emitted was barely audible. Stephen leaned his ear over Thori's mouth.

"*Skiiiaa-maahkia*," he said.

The sound was expelled like the end of life. Thori's head sank down in his pillow. The doctor moved Stephen aside to check his patient's pulse.

"He is resting," the doctor adjusted the top sheet. "You can wait outside if you want. It should not be long."

CHAPTER 45

On the verandah, several of the men napped on mattresses of blankets. Stephen squatted in the shade against one wall, cool on his back, and listened to their snores. Emotionally fatigued by the day, he too fell asleep with his head resting on his knees. It was so deep a sleep he would have been out for hours if the sun not had altered its position and burned its rays directly on his eyes. He woke parch-throated and collected the last glass of water on the tray and drank half its contents even though it had been sitting in the sun. Two old men, who sat close by Stephen, one quietly fiddling with his *komboloi* string of worry beads and the other smoking a pungent Greek cigarette, nodded to him as he reclaimed his spot.

"Do not finish your water," said the man with the *komboloi*. "Spill it in the yard and refill it from the pitcher. It has ice."

"Good idea, thank you," said Stephen

"When you went inside, did you see Thori?" inquired the second man.

"Yes."

"How was he?"

"Sleeping when I left."

The two men exchanged grave glances.

"Are you friends of Thori's?" said Stephen.

"Cousins. Why do you ask?"

"I was wondering how close you might be to him."

"Cousins," he repeated as though the word was a sufficient explanation. "Why does it matter?"

"Thori mentioned something to me but never explained it. I thought if you knew him well he might have told you."

"What was it?"

"A word that sounded like sciamacy."

The second man tossed his cigarette butt in the yard and deferred to his relative.

"Yes," said the first man, fingering his beads, "once Thori told me about sciamacy."

"What does it mean?" the second man saved Stephen the trouble of asking.

"Ah," the first man cleverly began, "that I cannot say. I can only tell you what Thori told me it meant. That could be different from the meaning other people give it."

"I would like to know Thori's interpretation," said Stephen.

"So," the first man leaned his elbows on the chair arms holding his *komboloi* with both fists and slowly passing one bead at a time from thumb to thumb, "it was last at the beginning of spring. Thori had just returned from a village in the northern part of the island. He had gone there on business; I can't remember the details."

"*Retsina*," the second man reminded.

"That's right; he went to buy *retsina* from a farmer who makes only two barrels a year. The perfect blend of wine and resin, he said. He had ridden there, leaving Thira at dawn on one of his son-in-laws mules, and it was evening when he returned. He was passing my house, which is just over there," he pointed, "and saw me sitting out front and decided to visit. We were close as children. Or maybe he didn't want to go home."

Stephen enjoyed the narrative, with all its asides, much as he wished he would get to the point. Like many old Greek men with little to do except converse in coffeehouses, he had his own way of relating an event. Urgency, for him, did not exist.

"My wife, who is a good woman, brought out food and wine and left us alone. For hours we drank and reminisced and that is when he told me about sciamacy."

"What did he say?" urged the second man.

"Thori was a knowledgeable man, though only the Devil knows how he acquired his wisdom. *Sciamacy*, he said, is one of the oldest words in our language. It was coined by the ancients, who possessed clarity of vision and were therefore the wisest men who ever lived, to explain the enigma of life. What was that? I asked him and these were almost his exact words: That a man during his lifetime must constantly wage a battle against invisible, incomprehensible, shadow forces until he is finally destroyed by them."

"What forces?" the second man asked and lit another cigarette.

"All he would say was that they are vicious, unrelenting forces that refuse to give even the most peace loving man a moment's peace. They have the power to suck the air out of lungs."

His account completed, the narrator relaxed in his chair. The second man struggled to make sense of what he had heard.

"But did not the death of our Savior change all that?"

"I asked nearly the same question," said the narrator.

"What did he tell you?"

"Nothing."

"Nothing?"

"He pinched my cheek and laughed."

Stephen lowered his head onto his knees. Soon a wave of moaning swept through the living room. The doctor appeared on the verandah to inform the men that, "Thori will never open his eyes again." The men who were awake stirred those who still slept. Some took out black armbands from their pockets and pushed them up their sleeves to their biceps. Another waved the children over to him and said, "The time has come, he is dead."

Stephen remained squatted on the floor with the ants until the verandah had cleared and everyone had entered the house to offer their condolences. Then he left.

CHAPTER 46

The miracle of life again proved as transient as a dream. If Thori's death had an impact on Stephen it was to remind him of his swim at Kamari beach, the day he had nearly drowned, and to confirm the reality of mortality. At Thori's house he had felt a detached observer of a play that had been performed for his singular edification. He wanted to endow sciamacy, as a deathbed declaration, with significance; but why should the last word a man utters be of any more value than his first babyish utterance of mama or dada?

In the alleys, Stephen became disoriented and chose his turns haphazardly not caring where they led. He felt like a rat in a maze, not of his making, seeking a reward, not of his choosing. He came out of the alleys in the square near the *souvlaki* stand. Not having eaten all day, the aroma of sizzling lamb tantalized his senses. Nancy and Jill were sitting at one of the sidewalk tables. He ordered several skewers and a large bottle of Fix beer and sat down with them.

"I'll never again complain about the English weather," said Nancy, as though they had been together all day. "It's so bloody hot it's positively depressing."

Stephen was too hungry to make small talk or even pay attention to their discussion of future plans. He finished his meal and lit a cigarette and sat back to enjoy the rest of his beer.

"Can you spare a fag?" asked Jill.

He handed her his cigarette and lit another.

"Have a piece," Jill offered him a slice of the watermelon they were eating.

"Do," said Nancy, "it's cool and sweet and will help relieve our guilt."

"What guilt is that?" he asked.

"For having inconsiderately eaten all your blood oranges the other day."

"A small slice then, but only to purge you conscience."

"A bargain," Nancy shook his hand to seal it.

"I'm glad you appeared," Jill set his slice on a paper napkin, "it's like meeting an old friend. Isn't it odd, I haven't seen you since yesterday and that seems like a year? We've known you for five days and seems like forever."

"It's this island; it obliterates one's sense of time and routine. Or maybe it's seeing a familiar face among strangers," Nancy conjectured.

"No doubt," said Stephen.

"Have you found any excitement?" Jill asked him.

"No."

"Is there anything on this island that could be called exciting?" Nancy wondered. "We've gone to the beach every day except yesterday out of boredom."

"Can we get together tonight?" asked Jill.

Stephen's mind was elsewhere and he did not answer.

"It's our last night. We're leaving tomorrow with Tom and Neal."

"We're leaving alright but not with them," said Nancy.

"Do say."

"Jill be realistic. We haven't seen them all day and for all we know they might have already left on this morning's ship."

"In the direction of India?" Stephen asked.

"To Athens then Spain."

"I suppose not everyone who journeys to the East makes it," said Stephen.

"What about tonight?" Jill prodded. "I thought we might eat in the place we went to the night we arrived. Remember that old man who got Nancy drunk? We could by him some wine. You think he'd like that?"

"I'm sure he would but I don't think you should count on his being there tonight," said Stephen. "The taverna will probably be closed. Repairs."

"What's in a place, we'll eat in the other taverna. We can meet there after dark and that will give us enough time to find Neal and Tom. If we find them fine, it not it can be the three of us. Let's make a good night of it."

"If I can," Stephen picked up his watermelon and stood to leave.

"Why can't you be honest? What you mean is, if you feel like it. Nothing could keep you from joining us if you cared to be there."

CHAPTER 47

Why should he care? He left a trail of watermelon seeds up March 25 Street and finished his fruit on the top stair of Rue Marinatos where he paused directionless. There was no reason for moving or for standing still.

Down the alley to his left was a half constructed building extending over the cliff. He felt compelled to see the view from its roof but there were no stairs or ladder. He had to scale the building using holes in the masonry and a thin ledge for hand and footholds. A fall would have been fatal. He hugged the wall like the abdomen of a woman. His thoughts reduced to the rush of adrenalin induced by the sound of dislodged stones or gravel somersaulting to the bottom of the cliff.

From atop, the whitewashed buildings of Thira's face sparkled in the sunlight as if they had been sprinkled with diamond chips. He stood at the edge of the roof above a sheer drop to the sea. The effect was dizzying. He felt a god looking down on the world from *the peaks and golden snows of Mount Olympus.* The blue sky merged with the clouds so far in the distance they appeared level with his eyes; a white plain that bore directly to the heart of the universe. The sea was a mirror reflection of the pure yellow of the sun.

Arms out stretched, he was engulfed by wind and could hear no sound that did not belong to it. He felt exhilarated. Wind through his clothing filled him with the sensation of flight. In his imagination he soared above the earth unfettered of its bonds, a sea eagle surfing the updrafts. He felt a unity and belonging with the universe. He felt caught up in the insular current of a river of energy. All that was required to confirm that reality was to step off and fly.

"NO," he had to shout to break the spell, but the wind stole his voice.

He lurched back onto the roof and lay motionless until he regained his breath and senses. When he braved another look over the edge, what he saw was a cliff and a blue sea, reality as obvious as death. At that moment Thori died for him.

He discovered a safer way off the roof but felt compelled to return the way he had come to round out the experience and give the fates another shot. When he stood on firm ground again he felt invigorated,

I am whole and sound and to hell with the rest.

He needed something of consequence to do. Anything. There was no point in returning to Akrothiri. He thought about finding Jill to try and purge Danielle from his mind, but the prospect of separating her from Nancy presented too many obstacles. By the time that could be accomplished he would probably have thought better of it.

He would return to his room and work on his poetry. Lines from his work passed through his head. He moved encapsulated in Erato's dimension without the delusion of having severed the bonds of this one.

In the vicinity of his room, he turned up an alley of stairs taking them two at a time. There was a young man loitering up top who waited until Stephen was committed to his ascent before starting down.

Couldn't the son-of-a-bitch have waited a few more seconds?

Midway they met. The narrow space restricted their passing and Stephen leaned back against the wall expecting the young man to do the same. Instead, he caught a glimmer of light reflected off metal and looked at its source in time to see a knife thrust up at him. Twisting to dodge its path, Stephen pushed out his arm for protection. His hand caught the assailant's wrist but the force of the thrust implanted the blade in his side.

The stranger hesitated, seemingly terrified at what he had done, and released the blade. Blood began to stain Stephen's shirt as he clenched the knife handle and tore it from his flesh. He became simultaneously aware of his injury's pain and a woman's voice shouting,

"Murder."

Stephen slipped to his knees and looked up at his assailant wondering the reason for the attack and why he didn't finish the job. The confused, contorted features of the face he saw seemed vaguely familiar. Before he could place him, his assailant bolted and ran.

"Murder," the woman's voice continued.

"Where?" a man's voice responded.

"There."

"I see nothing."

"Blind man, come down with me," she ordered.

The shock of the experience caused Stephen to lose sense of time. There was no telling how long he remained on his knees, clutching his side, before help arrived. The first person to reach him was the old woman.

"I saw it from up there," she said. "Are you hurt badly?"

Stephen held his side as though pressure would staunch the wound.

"He is alive," said the man who had taken the old woman's cry of murder as a statement of fact.

"You have eyes after all," said the old woman. "Get him to his feet."

Another man arrived at the scene.

"Can you walk?" the old woman asked.

Stephen relied on the wall to get to his feet but was too unsteady to walk

"Put his arm about your shoulder," she instructed the man.

"Where are we taking him?" he asked her.

"To his room."

"Where is that?"

"Up there next to mine. You go fetch the doctor," she ordered a second man who had arrived at the scene.

"And a policeman," added the man who was helping Stephen.

"The doctor first," she insisted. "If he is not in his office try Kyrie Thori's house."

"You can make it," the man encouraged Stephen.

Slowly, one step at a time they made it to the room. Stephen eased himself onto his bed and gave the man a pack of Viceroy's in gratitude.

"Go now," the old woman ushered the Samaritan from the room. "The doctor is coming; I'll wait for him outside."

Stephen studied the knife he still clutched in his hand. It was a green-handled stiletto and he set it on the nightstand and waited.

CHAPTER 48

"Where is he?" asked a voice in the courtyard.

"In there doctor," Kyria Rhea directed.

"Will you need me doctor?" asked the Samaritan.

"No, yes it might be best if you stayed."

The door opened just enough to admit the doctor.

"You should have stayed at Thori's house with the other mourners," he said when he recognized his patient.

"The thought's crossed my mind."

"Is this the weapon?" he checked the knife blade.

"Yes."

"What happened? Never mind, it makes no difference to me."

He unbuttoned Stephen's shirt to view the wound and pressed the tender area

"Does this hurt?"

Stephen gritted his teeth to mitigate the pain. The doctor left the bedside to collect his bag and dismiss the man who waited in the courtyard.

"So I am not in such bad shape after all," Stephen felt reassured enough to say.

"The bleeding has stopped. There are no internal injuries; the blade did not penetrate that deep. You removed the knife yourself?"

"Yes."

"That was foolish; you could have caused more damage. Remain still again, the wound must be cleansed. It will sting."

Burn would have been a better description. The pain teared Stephen's eyes.

"You need three stitches. I have something to numb the pain."

Stephen gritted his teeth again.

"You have a high threshold for pain," said the doctor, absorbed in his work. "Leave the sutures; they will come out on their own. I will put on a bandage and leave you some antiseptic and gauze to change it a couple times a day. If you leave Santorini, you should have a physician check it in a few days. If the wound bleeds or if the pain becomes intense have it checked immediately. You have been very lucky. How do you feel, weak?"

"Not energetic."

"Stay in bed the rest of the night. Do not move any more than necessary to use the bathroom or get a drink. I will have the old woman bring something mild for dinner. These pills are for the pain and this for sleep if you need it."

"Doctor, there is a policeman here," said Kyria Rhea from the other side of the door.

"Have him wait. Did you send for a policeman?" he asked Stephen.

"No."

"Have you decided what story to tell him?"

"Story?" The word implied Stephen had something to hide.

"Well?"

"You think I precipitated this?"

"Roll up your sleeve," he dropped the issue. "I am going to give you shots of tetanus and penicillin. Are you allergic to either of them?"

"No."

The doctor measured out the syringes and administered them.

"I will check on you in the morning," he said, closing up his medical bag.

"That won't be necessary. Just take what I owe you."

Stephen's wallet was on the nightstand. The doctor took his fee.

"I can pay your usual charge," said Stephen, surprised by the modest cost. He did not want to be indebted to someone who assumed the worst of his character without the benefit of knowing him.

"I am a physician. My business is saving lives, not becoming another Onassis even when days like this make me regret I chose this profession."

"Yes, it was too bad about Thori," said Stephen.

"Not Thori. His death was expected. His drinking was suicidal. It is not Thori or you who are well enough that upsets me. It is the young woman."

"Who?"

"A Canadian."

"Esther," Stephen volunteered a name, "with curly hair?"

"You knew her?"

"Knew?"

"She is dead."

"When?"

"About dawn."

"How?"

"She was on the roof of one of the houses that overhang the cliff. Either she fell by accident or on purpose."

"Murder?"

"You have a sinister mind. Suicide. Perhaps you could settle the issue, did you know her well?"

How well was well? Stephen suddenly realized it was Laki who attacked him.

The doctor was leaving.

"Could you put the policeman off?" Stephen asked.

Guessing his assailant, he wanted time to think. The doctor gave him a look that seemed to say you must have something to hide. The policeman stepped into the room as soon as the door opened.

"I do not want my patient disturbed Yanni," the doctor addressed him by name.

"I must make a report."

"Nothing very serious as you can see for yourself. It is important for him to rest and I have given him something to make him sleep."

"The old woman said something about murder."

"Murder," the doctor forced a laugh and put his arm about the officer's shoulder and gestured senility.

The policeman seemed relieved.

"I will come and tell you about it tomorrow," said Stephen.

The officer left with the doctor.

Chapter 49

Esther dead. Poor Esther.

What a hypocrite you've become, Stephen thought of himself in the third person. Why poor Esther? Because she committed suicide? Is it better to die when you desire death rather than have your life stolen from you when you have reason to live?

"Laki tried to kill me," he mumbled as though hearing the words would make them believable. "It's insane."

No, not insane. Everything is, period, even if it isn't.

The sullenness of his mood affected his thoughts.

I was blind and deaf last night. Thori wasn't drinking for fun or escape; he was shadow boxing his invisible forces for his life. Esther had no ulterior motive for coming home with me save a reason to exist, or for the distraction to forget she couldn't find one. I let her down on both accounts. I was too busy drinking *tsipouro* and wanting Danielle who could never be whatever I imagine her to be.

They were joyless thoughts. He would retreat into his poetry. The manila envelope was on the nightstand and he leafed through its pages. Its images offered neither pleasure nor distraction. He flung the envelope across the room.

He lay in bed until the saturnine pall of evening when Kyria Rhea brought him bread and cheese and olives and a bottle of water. She did not speak to Stephen then or when she returned accompanied by a man who man stood in the shadows by the door until she left the room.

When he approached the light about the bed, Stephen recognized him as Laki's father. Esther had pointed Loutras out the night he had met Danielle at the Hotel Atlantis. His face was somber and he wore a black suit and bore himself like a man afflicted by the weight of the world.

"I am..." he began with difficulty.

"Laki's father."

"You know my son?"

"By sight alone."

The man stooped his shoulders visibly disheartened.

"This has been a day of agony," he said. "Dear Virgin, what senseless tragedy."

Stephen pitied the man his plight but prepared himself for the confrontation. Be aware of yourself, he thought, and what has been done to you.

"There is a chair over there," he pointed.

Loutras repositioned it by the bed. The chair was in a dilapidated state and the caution with which he eased himself on it would have been humorous in other circumstances.

"I spoke with the doctor," he extended his hand to touch Stephen's forearm, "how are you?"

"If you spoke with him you know."

"He said it was more painful than serious. I want to pay your medical expenses," he reached inside his jacket for his wallet in a businesslike manner.

"I already settled accounts with him."

"Then allow me to reimburse you," Loutras spread out some bills enticingly on the nightstand.

"No."

"For your suffering."

"Not if I was down to my last drachma."

"If you should have second thoughts…" Loutras re-pocketed the money. "Kyrie Stephanos, I am a man who speaks frankly in all matters. You know it was my son who stabbed you."

"You know I do."

"Have you spoken to the police about the accident?"

"Accident? Laki tried to kill me. A policeman visited earlier but I put him off until tomorrow."

"Then I have arrived in time, thank God," Loutras dabbed his forehead. "I have come to plea for my son's life."

"By reducing the value of mine to a handful of drachmas and paying me off," said Stephen and imagined Priam pleading with Achilles for Hector's body.

"No. You misunderstand my motives. You are Greek I am told."

"Sometimes. Sometimes not."

"No, no," Loutras rejected the qualification. "I am speaking of blood not identification papers, passports."

So this is how one barters for a human life, Stephen thought. He didn't bat an eyelash when I turned down his money. I wonder if he'll convince me.

"My son was not responsible for what has happened to you. It is the girl who is to blame."

"Esther, how can you possibly blame her? She is dead."

"Dead yes and it is sadness and I will not speak ill of the dead. I am a widower with one child, a son. You are young and carefree and cannot appreciate the meaning of parenthood. One day you will."

"I doubt it."

"Yes you will. It is the way of the earth. It is the seed of that is nurtured our minds and roots in our groins. To have a son, how can I expect you to understand?" Loutras shook his head. "If you tell the police Laki tried to kill you he will be sent to prison. Not forever, a year. At my age a year is a short period but for a young man it is an eternity and its effects can be lethal. Can I have your word that you will not report him?."

What to say? To allow Laki to go unpunished would be to confess his own life was valueless. That in itself was not difficult to accept but inherent in that confession would be that another's life had more intrinsic value than his own. All men were equal in the only respect that mattered, the possession of life; equal in value or valuelessness, a balance to be preserved.

Loutras interpreted Stephen's silence as a rejection of his appeal. He took a different tact.

"From the day she arrived on Santorini she took possession of Laki and would not give him peace. She hounded him like a witch, kept his life in turmoil, smothered his soul with her demands and need for him. Though she is dead, she will destroy him from the grave."

"Thori liked her," said Stephen, remembering the Esther he had known and not the one Loutras conjured.

"That drunkard liked anyone who would waste a moment with him," Loutras replied.

"I thought you were not going to speak ill of the dead."

"This is not easy for me," Loutras regained his composure. "I do not wish to disrespect the dead but the truth must be known for my son's sake. You do not know Laki but ask anyone who does and they will tell of his great compassion for people. It was in keeping with his generous nature that he befriended Esther. But she took advantage. Laki is not wise about women. She convinced him that he loved her, made him believe he could love no other woman, though she was unfaithful to him. In spite of evidence I gathered, he would not believe it. And then this morning because she understood that Laki had outgrown his need for her, and to punish him, she killed herself. She was not well, how could a sane person throw oneself off a cliff? Laki could not understand. To him his love had died without reason. Someone told him she had been with you last night. In his bereavement he blamed you for her death. It was not Laki but her manipulation of him that did this to you."

Incredible, thought Stephen. Incredible if it's true, incredible that someone would make up such a story if it isn't.

"If you tell the police that what happened was an accident, they won't question you."

There was a knock at the door.

"Stephen," said a male voice in the courtyard. "It's me."

"Hold on," said Stephen.

"Will you give me your hand in agreement?" Loutras asked.

"I'll wait as long as you want if you'll just tell me where there's a john out here," said Neal.

"It's in here," said Stephen.

"Then I'll have to ask you to hurry up. You might say it's an emergency. Who've you got in there anyway, Hedy Lamarr or Bridget Bardot?"

"Come on in," Stephen said.

"Sorry," Neal said when he saw Loutras.

"In there," Stephen pointed and said to Loutras, "go on, he does not speak Greek."

"I will have your answer," Loutras took up his hat and prepared to leave.

"You will, when I have thought it through."

"Whatever I must do to protect my son..."

"For your son's sake be careful who you threaten. You never know how many people might already know the truth," Stephen cast a glance toward the bathroom and the sound of Neal relieving himself.

"I have said what had to be said Kyrie Stephanos, you know my meaning. Who do you imagine the police would believe me or your friend? Good night."

Loutras had played his gambit well: first the bribe, then the appeal, finally the threat.

A man of experience, Stephen mused.

Chapter 50

Stephen was not in a sociable mood but he had to admit that Neal's appearance had been opportune. It gave him time. He could not pass judgment on Laki and his side ached with the slightest move. He took the pill the doctor had prescribed and began to feel its effects.

"That man leave on my account?" asked Neal.

"No."

"Good, I'm a sensitive person. Odd looking man, I don't know the word I want, yes I do, desperate. Hell with it, shall we go?"

"Where to?"

"The taverna. Tom and the girls are waiting. Jill said it had been settled. We're all leaving tomorrow and supposed to celebrate our departure. But, lest I forget," Neal took out his pipe, "let us straighten out our minds before seeing to our stomachs."

"Portrait of the pusher pushing his merchandise."

Neal laughed.

"You know, the girls took me seriously when I told them that was my profession. I just thought pusher pushing eastward had more flair to it than law student who refuses to finish his degree."

"It does have a certain ring to it."

"Here," Neal proffered his pipe.

"Not tonight, thanks."

"What do you mean; it's like a farewell to here and now; just as a symbolic gesture."

"You're right."

"Yeah, I should never have made up that story. Nancy's constantly glaring into my eyes. Those girls are a strange pair."

"How's that?"

"Nancy's too, too tense. She gives me the feeling that she might flip out at any second. Did you make it with Jill?"

"Why?"

"She came on strong in the beginning first with me and then Tom but neither of us got her all the way into bed. We think they're having some sort of relationship. We caught them in bed together. They said they were playing, but under the sheets? If it was a game it was a strange one. You think?"

"I don't think anything would surprise me."

"Chicks, what a mess. The system's all screwed up. When I was fifteen I was so hungry for a woman I could have made it with a dozen of them twenty-four hours a day. But could I get one? When the urge is there, they're not. As sex becomes more complicated, there they are with all their neuroses and psychoses. Which is worse, being able to handle them anywhere, any time and not being able to get one or being able to get as many as you want but only being able to enjoy them at certain times?"

"They told me you and Tom were heading back to Italy."

"Just passing through. We want to get back to the States by mid September and we're thinking about blowing the rest of our roll in Amsterdam on good times."

"Pipe's out," Stephen said.

"Refill?"

"Not for me."

"Shall we go?"

"I can't make it tonight."

"Why?"

Stephen unbuttoned his shirt.

"What happened to you?" Neal asked about the bandages.

Stephen pointed to the knife on the nightstand.

"I knew there was something the matter when you didn't show up. Jill said it was because you didn't want to but I decided to look for you. Only problem was nobody knew where you were staying. Then I ran into our landlord."

"Trekas," Stephen had to force his eyelids to remain open.

"Is that his name? I got him to bring me half way here and point out the place. Jill was going to come along but, you met a girl named Esther didn't you?"

"Yes."

"Nancy heard that she'd been murdered and is afraid there's a killer loose on the island. She wouldn't let Jill leave her alone. So, Tom stayed with them."

"Esther killed herself. She jumped off the cliff."

"No kidding? Anybody know why?"

"Anyone's guess."

"How are you? Would you like me to get the others?"

"No. I'd appreciate it if you didn't mention this to Nancy and Jill. It's nothing and I'll be fine by morning. I just need some sleep and I took a pill the doctor gave me and its beginning to wipe me out."

"How did it happen?"

"Just did. When are you leaving tomorrow?"

"The one o'clock ship, but you never know for sure until it arrives."

"I'll stop by in the morning to say good-bye."

"Good enough, but what if they ask me about you?"

"Tell them I had to see someone or that I wasn't here."

"Nothing else?" Neal took his cue to leave from Stephen's yawns.

"Not that I can think of."

"It's a shame about Esther, isn't it?"

CHAPTER 51

It was an unusually cold night. An unseasonable rain fell on Santorini, lashed by a tempestuous wind. It blew open Stephen's window with a crash that startled him from a sound sleep.

Awake, he became aware of aching joints and a burning forehead. The induction of the cool air swept and cooled his face and he nearly succumbed again to the medicinal oblivion of sleep. But his body was drenched with perspiration that was chilled until it felt like ice on his flesh. His wound throbbed and movement was painful.

With a hand pressed against his side, he got out of bed and latched the window tight. Turning round, the room swam in waves before his eyes, fading almost white in the darkness. A quiver, born in his spine, electrified his muscles with shivers that caused him to lean against the wall for support. His heart pounded so hard against his chest he feared it would burst and spew a river of blood bubbling out his parched throat. He wished he could pass out but his mind remained sober to his becoming surreal surroundings and a delirium of thoughts.

There was a knock at the door.

"Who is it?" said Stephen.

"Loutras."

"I'm not feeling well, go away."

"Open the door; I have come for your decision or your life."

"I have a gun," Stephen threatened.

He waded through the dark to the dresser and felt for his flight bag. The pounding continued. He withdrew his revolver.

"Who do you think you are to take my son from me?"

"I'll shoot."

The door shook with such violence it seemed about to be torn from its hinges. Stephen aimed the gun. A bolt of lightning lit up the room, a peal of thunder shook the foundation with such a trauma of noise it deadened the sound of the shot. The pounding stopped. The storm abated and there was stillness, save the subtle rhythm of raindrops.

I killed him, Stephen thought, and though he wanted to inspect his victim he fell wearily onto the bed. He propped his back up against pillows and sat with the gun in his lap, eyes on the door. Did he sleep? There was a gentler tapping at the door.

"I will shoot," he reissued his warning.

"No," said a softer voice. "I've come to save you."

"Danielle," the silhouette was unmistakable.

A hand reached out to him but the figure he drew close was Esther not Danielle

"You could have saved me," she whispered, "but you let me die. You let me die and refuse to punish those who drove me to my death."

"Let him be," said Barba. "He is one of God's creatures and no more perfect than any other."

"God's creature," Thori laughed. "Like all of us he is but a blemish on the face of this volcano-talking god of yours. Listen to no one but me friend and judge the truth of what I say. Today you set off to meet with love but what did you find instead?"

"Emptiness," said Esther.

"Shadows," Thori corrected. "You reach for love on this earth and you find bodies for distraction."

"Come, I have such a soft, warm, moist tightness with which to satisfy you," Esther imitated Jill's voice seductively.

"If you had drowned at Kamari beach who but the fish would have known or cared? Those beauties beneath the shade eating your blood oranges?" said Thori.

Esther shook her head.

"Of what value are any of us? What does your presence on this earth one day more or less matter? You fight only to lose and from now on pain and disappointment will exceed the pleasure. What do you see in the mirror?"

"The last flicker of youth," said Esther, "the last illusion of knowledge and immortality."

"You will live only to witness your body rot off its frame like overcooked meat. Torture is the price of prolonged survival. When we find the courage to face our worthlessness what do we cry out for?"

"God," said Barba.

"Oblivion," Thori pointed to the gun. "You are dead already and only the death of death can give you the freedom you desire."

"You know you have been considering it for some time," said Esther. "Isn't that why you came to Santorini?"

Stephen pressed the gun barrel against his temple and...

SATURDAY

CHAPTER 52

A SCREAM.

Stephen opened his eyes to the barrel of his gun aimed at his face. When a hand probed his ribs, he stirred.

"You're alive," a voice said.

Half asleep, he took in the blurred figure of a woman hovering over him. Her perfume and the outline of her nipples through her cotton dress made him think it was Jill. But it was Nancy.

"Give me that," she took the gun from his hand. "God what a fright. I thought you were dead. Have you any idea what discovering a dead body can do to a person? Look," she stretched out her trembling arm, "I haven't been so shaken since, please say something."

"Since you were hissed at in a dark alley," said Stephen and wiped the sleep from his eyes.

"Even that wasn't as bad as this."

"What brings you?"

"You needn't be cross."

"It's not every morning I'm awakened by a scream."

"It's not every morning you look a corpse. I came because I was concerned about you and to bring you these." Nancy held up a paper bag then poured its contents onto the bed. "Pomegranates. I had a time getting them. Most of the shops are closed. Half the town appears dressed for a funeral. They wouldn't be burying Esther would they?"

"Unlikely. Officials have to notify the Canadian Embassy and let them contact her family first, see if the family wants done with the body. Have the church bells rung for any length of time?"

"No more than usual."

"Are you and Jill leaving today?"

"In a few hours. I have to get back and wake her. We still have to pack. There are two ships scheduled to arrive within a few hours of each other and ours is the first. The one to Mykonos and Athens."

"You'll have Tom and Neal for company."

"Their plans have changed. They met some Australian blokes with tents and gear last night and they're all going to camp out at the beach for a few days. To party as Neal puts it. That's why this morning before they left he told me about what happened to you."

"I told him not to," Stephen thought out loud.

"Only because he wanted Jill and me to know in case you didn't come to say good-bye and not to assume it was because you didn't care to, or didn't like us. It was considerate of him," said Nancy. "Stephen, can I speak with you, seriously?"

"After I've showered. I won't be conscious until I do. Maybe you can change this bandage for me."

"How are you?"

"Having survived last night I feel alright at the moment."

"Was it that bad? Neal didn't give any details."

"I take quick showers. Squeeze the pomegranates."

Chapter 53

"Tight, loose?" asked Nancy.

"Perfect. You'll make a good nurse."

"I can rewrap it if it's not right."

Stephen shook his head.

"You could have left the other bandage on," said Nancy, inspecting it and rolling the gauze into its cylinder.

"I needed that cool shower."

"Now you feel baptized," Nancy smiled, "cleansed of sickness and sin."

"Very good, "Stephen bit into the reddest pomegranate and sucked its juice. "Sweet. You have a talent for picking them. What did you want to talk to me about?"

"When will you be leaving Santorini?"

"Who knows?" Stephen sat down on the edge of the bed. "When the mood strikes."

"Come with us today."

"Sorry, I don't feel in a travel mood."

"We need you."

"Need," Stephen discarded the pomegranate for a cigarette, "now that's a very interesting word. Lately I've become somewhat expert in its use. I needed a girl but survived without her. Did I need? A girl needed me yet even if had satisfied her passing need it wouldn't have been the need she needed. So what is need? Can it ever apply to anything but food and water? What the hell could you possibly need me for Nancy?"

"Disregarding me, there's Jill."

"And she definitely is a girl who needs whoever."

"How unkind you are. I suppose I should expect that attitude from a man. We give ourselves to you and get denigrated in return. But before you have us how special we are, never have you seen such eyes or lips."

"You're putting words and attitudes in my mouth. I don't care who people sleep with. I'm indifferent. What I meant by who was…"

"I understood you right enough."

"I doubt it," Stephen walked to the dresser, "but since you assume you do there's nothing left to say. You should get back to Jill."

Stephen took out a clean shirt from the top drawer. He kept his back to Nancy, expecting to hear the door close behind her, but she remained seated.

"Well?" he turned and saw her cradling his gun like a prized possession. "You're clutching my gun like your life depended on it."

"It's not unnatural for a person to contemplate suicide," she said.

"Is that why you're holding the gun, you plan to use it? Or do you think I am?"

"I was thinking of Esther. Everyone experiences periods of despair but they pass."

"Sometimes not soon enough" said Stephen.

"Sometimes it seems like never."

"Your divorce," Stephen recalled their conversation on Kamari beach and braced for a verbal assault on the nature of men.

Nancy shook her head.

"What then? Go on, we'll probably never see each other again after today anyway."

"I've been trying to forget it."

"But you haven't forgotten and you'll tell me because you feel the need to, so stop tormenting yourself," he said, wishing he had not gotten into the conversation and wondering how to get out of it.

"I murdered my baby," Nancy said and began to sob.

"You said you never had children, remember? Are you talking about an abortion, is that it? You had an abortion and feel guilty about it?"

He had an answer for that one but she didn't answer him and he idly watched the agonized convulsing of her chest and tears drip from her lashes like beads of moisture off a leaf.

"I'm sorry for this," Nancy cleared her throat and wiped away the tears with the back of her hand, "but you demand to know all don't you, and so you will."

"You don't owe me an explanation, really, I was just making conversation."

"No, I have to tell someone. I wasn't completely truthful when we talked on the beach. I did love my husband, which was true. He abused me and that was true. But I left out the baby. My baby was going to give my life meaning and win back his affection. I conceived her without his knowledge or approval. One night he came home drunk. He had been with another woman again to forget me and my condition as he described it. I hadn't heard from him for days and I was hurt and angry. We quarreled and he hit me," Nancy wiped her eyes again, "and I lost my daughter."

"That makes it his fault not yours," Stephen tried to console her.

"No. I never saw him again after that night. In hospital, with tubes in my arm, I could not get it out of my mind that I had murdered my baby, as though I had plotted her death."

"That's a pretty extreme conclusion don't you think?" he asked and wondered what to make of her story.

"You don't live with a man and not understand his temperament. I knew what could happen if I confronted him that night. I should have remembered my condition and what I had to lose. My nightmare is that my subconscious wanted him to kill our child so that he would be tormented to his grave; as if he could care."

"You believe that?"

"After I was released from hospital I couldn't cope with what I'd done. For months I kept very much alone, unable to tolerate men even as casual acquaintances. I wanted to die. My only pleasure came from thinking about how to end my life, but I couldn't do it."

He wanted to ask her what methods she had considered.

"At university I met Jill. For her own reasons, she was floundering like me and we became, well, we needed each other. She saved my life."

"How so?"

"By convincing her flat mates to let me move in with them. I don't know what might have happened if I'd been alone much longer. That's why this Esther thing has me so upset…I didn't know her but I can understand why she could have taken her life."

Stephen waited but Nancy had nothing further to say. Buttoning his shirt, he saw his face reflected in the mirror. It seemed callous and alien to him. Maybe he should grow a beard?

A solitary church bell tolled.

"Do you still want me to leave with you and Jill?" he asked.

"Yes," she looked at him to see if he was being sincere. "We have two more weeks in Greece and as strangers in a foreign country it can be trying. We used to be able to help each other but our relationship has changed. We both need someone and we both trust you."

"If, and I mean if, we travel together it must be understood that I'm free to part company whenever and without explanations."

"But you wouldn't just abandon us?

"No, not that."

"Agreed."

"I have a matter to settle before I can leave so I can't promise to go with you. I may not have time to catch the ship."

"I could do your packing now," Nancy volunteered.

"That would help, especially if you'd take my bags down the cliff with you. If I'm not in time to catch the ship just leave them at the café. Don't forget that," he pointed to the manila envelope that still lay on the floor where he had tossed it.

Nancy picked it up.

"The gun," he held out his hand.

Stephen wedged the gun securely inside his belt and put on a jacket to conceal it and stepped out into the pellucid sunlight.

Chapter 54

Stephen paused in the courtyard to knock at Kyria Rhea's door. He wanted to thank her and leave her some money. There was no response and the bells were calling so he did not linger.

In the wake of the storm, a brilliant rainbow arched a frame over the sea beyond the volcano like a positive omen. The air smelled clean and fresh and pools of rainwater in the streets rippled in the breeze. Ascending the southern end of the cliff wall, he could see the church above him. It was whitewashed like most of the island's two hundred and fifty churches and chapels and the feature that identified it from the rest was its blue dome.

Mourners were taking their seats as Stephen arrived. He lit a candle in memory of Kyrie Thori but did not cross himself nor kiss the icon of Mary holding the infant Jesus. Beyond the vestibule, the church was so crowded that Stephen had to lean against the back wall. He looked about for Barba but instead encountered Thori's cousin, who had imparted the meaning of sciamacy, and they exchanged expressions of solemnity.

Thori's coffin had been laid before the purple-clothed altar of God. On either side of it, life-size icons stood like bodyguards. One was of Saint Irene, the island's patroness, and the other of Saint George slaying a dragon. On the circular ceiling a painting of the resurrected Christ balancing the world in his palm observed the assembly with an expression of benign perplexity.

Heads bowed and crossing themselves three times, the congregation rose to its feet when the black robed and bearded priest appeared. The service was delivered in a series of chants exchanged between the priest and two cantors, while the atmosphere thickened with the smoke of incense.

Stephen's mind drifted from the proceedings to Laki. The situation between them had to be redressed someway. Even by doing nothing he would be doing something. What an absurd situation.

Moments before Laki had attempted to steal his life he had nearly thrown it away, off the cliff, perhaps from the same spot Esther had ended hers. Did justice demand to be placated and what was justice?

The ecclesiastical portion of the ritual completed, the pall bearers bore Thori's coffin up the aisle. Stephen fell in at the end of line. Outside, the crowd waited for Iphigenia and her husband to find their proper place in the procession's hierarchy before moving toward the graveyard. There was little resemblance between the silent, sorrowful faces Stephen observed and the ones Thori had conjured in his portrayal of his funereal two nights ago. Barba was missing and if members were slandering the deceased's sacrilegious notions they kept it to themselves. Not a crow could be seen. The single point that Thori had prophesized correctly was Esther's absence.

As the mourners crossed April 21 Street, moving away from the periphery of town, Stephen saw Laki standing in front of his shop. He was in the company of two friends and the three were laughing and patting each other's backs. Laki was anything but the picture of a grieving lover.

Stephen dropped from the ranks of the funereal train and watched it straggle out of sight. He lit a cigarette and waited for Laki to be alone in his shop. Slipping his hand inside his jacket, he grasped the butt of his gun, unsure of what he had in mind. As he approached the shop he saw Kyrie Loutras at the far end of the street exit the Hotel Atlantis and paused long enough to be noticed by him. When he was convinced that Loutras sensed the danger his son was in and began rushing up the street, Stephen stepped into the shop.

Laki had his back to the door. He stood behind a display case arranging as assortment of inexpensive silver bracelets on a wall peg.

"So Laki," said Stephen, drawing out his gun.

Laki turned round to see Stephen framed in the doorway. A look of terror filled his face as the gun was pointed in his direction.

"My father explained," Laki appealed. "Is it more money..."

Stephen fired one shot. Laki dropped toppling the display case, shattering its glass, scattering its jewelry and worry beads and volcanic rocks across the floor.

Loutras arrived within seconds of the shot. He threw his arms about Stephen and squeezed his wounded side and wrested the gun from his unresisting grip. Once he had possession of the weapon, he hurried to his son's side.

"If he is dead," Loutras threatened but Laki began to stir.

"He tried to kill me," said Laki, taking measure of himself. "He's crazy."

"Where are you hit?" asked Loutras. "There's blood on your arm and forehead."

"Nowhere. I got cut when I fell through the case but I think I sprained my wrist," said Laki as his father helped him to his feet. "He tried to kill me."

"Laki must be confused," said Stephen. "I was showing him the gun when it fired, by accident."

"No! He aimed at me," and Laki tried to cock his fingers to imitate a gun until he felt the pain in his wrist.

"You are not going to get away with this," Loutras insisted. "I am sending for the police."

"I wouldn't Loutras," Stephen took out Laki's stiletto from his jean pocket and dangled it. "Notify the police or return my gun to me. I will be in café."

CHAPTER 55

There were no customers in the café. The proprietor and his mother were taking advantage of the lull by preparing for the day's anticipated influx of new arrivals. He replenished the stock of ice cream and drinks in the outdoor freezer while she positioned her stool behind the cash register.

Stephen sat indoors at the table from where he had observed Danielle arranging her visit to the volcano. Esther passed through his mind like a mirage, but his thoughts were occupied with Loutras and what he might do. He could image a number of scenarios including his arrival with the police or entering the café shooting. His thoughts were all over the place and he decided to try to focus them by writing a poem or anything. After all, the words could prove to be his last will and testament.

"Have you any paper?" he asked the proprietor's mother.

"We have three kinds of coffee: Greek, espresso, and Nescafe," the half-deaf woman replied.

"No, alright, *café au lait*," Stephen walked over to her, "but have you any paper?"

"What kind of paper?"

"Writing paper."

"Go to the kiosk in the square," she said.

"What about one of these?" he asked and thumbed through the four, thin, blue-covered booklets beside the register.

"My son keeps accounts in them."

"But all are blank. Shall I ask him? I would pay for one."

"What do you want it for?"

"I am writing an article about Santorini and where visitors should go to eat breakfast."

"Will you mention this café?"

"Is there a better one on the island? Have you a pencil I could borrow?"

She took one out of the drawer under the register.

"Three drachmas for the booklet and two-and-a-half for the coffee."

He paid her and took his coffee and booklet back to his table. It was pointless trying to write so he used the pages to draw geometric patterns. He had filled three of its five pages and there was no sign of Loutras so he ordered a Greek coffee and smoked a cigarette. Still no Loutras. He took up the pencil again and sketched the walls and buildings across the street, which was mindless enough to do because their lines gave shape to geometric forms. Looking up at one point, he finally saw Loutras in the street speaking with a policeman. They parted company and Loutras crossed to the café. He located Stephen, looked about to see that there were no other customers and sat at his table across from him. He glanced warily about as he returned Stephen his gun under the table. Stephen tucked it away.

"Laki's wrist needed medical attention," said Loutras. "I trust you didn't get nervous and go to the police."

"No I didn't and don't intend to."

"I want my son officially vindicated."

"Then vindicate him yourself. Because my bags were carried down the cliff for me, I have decided to leave on the next ship," Stephen checked his watch to learn that it was one-forty. "I've already missed the one I was planning to take."

"You have two hours until the next one so you still have time to clear up…"

"Not for that. In the end you will get your wish. I won't be here to identify Laki or press charges."

"I intend to take no chances."

"You should understand by now that chance is one of the wonders of life," Stephen folded the booklet and slipped it into his pocket and stood to leave.

"If circumstances were different…" Loutras struggled with his temper. "There is no excuse for what you did. Laki was bereaved."

"So you say."

"You think I lied to you last night? That girl was no good. Even I…"

"Go on. Why did Esther kill herself? Did she?"

"What are you implying?"

"Nothing, and there is nothing anyone can do about her now and besides what I am interested is the money."

"What money?"

"The money you offered me last night."

"I don't have it with me."

"I'll take whatever you have on you."

Loutras took out bills totaling several hundred drachmas, about thirty-six dollars.

"This is it, but if you imagine I would give it to you then you are insane."

"Insane enough to visit the police."

"After what you did today, if Laki goes to jail you will keep him company."

"You think that concerns me?"

"That gun should be used to put you out of your misery like a rabid dog."

"If you want to use it for that purpose I can return it to you. Make up your mind."

Loutras laid his money on the table. Stephen thought to explain to him that it wasn't the money but the principal but instead pocketed it without counting it.

"My pencil," the old woman said when she saw Stephen head toward the door. He pointed to where he had left the pencil and she let loose a string of invectives that followed him into the street.

Chapter 56

Atop Rue Marinatos, horses and donkeys were arriving with the latest assortment of tourists. Stephen found his landlord vying with other concierges for prospective renters and helped him convince two Danish girls to let his old room. He paid Renas what he owed him and made arrangements with his son for a ride down the cliff.

The hour before he had to descend to catch the second ship gave him time to say good-bye to Barba. Walking along the cliff path, he could see the Athens bound ship leaving the caldera and felt a degree of ambivalence about Nancy and Jill being on it.

Barba was standing in front of his shop smoking a cigarette and leaning on the cliff wall, entranced by his prospect of the volcano. He must have noticed Stephen because, although he retained his stare, when he turned to him he spoke as if they were in the midst of a conversation.

"Once each day I take the time to look at the old man out there and do not take my eyes off him until I am able to see him as he is when he erupts. That is a sight of pure power. He was the first to make me feel God. I was young then and before I saw him explode what did I know?"

"I am leaving on the next ship and came to wish you health and longevity."

"Longevity," he smiled.

"Longer longevity."

The old man laughed.

"Come into the shop, I want to make you a present for your trip."

"That is not necessary."

"I am not doing it because it is necessary but because you are respectful of an old man's feelings. Come in, come in. At my age there are only three pleasures: to see the morning sun, to embrace family and to make a gift to a friend. You are giving me the opportunity to enjoy the third."

The room was dark as usual. Stephen took the chair he had slept in his second night on Santorini.

"What kind of wine would you prefer? White? Personally, I believe that red wine is better for your blood but you are still young and can afford a few minor gambles," Barba handed a him a bottle of white wine. "Because you are leaving us today we must share a drink of my choice to assure a smooth voyage."

Barba poured two glasses of sweet, red Mavro Daphne wine.

"Did you meet her?"

"Who?" Stephen wondered.

"The young lady you told me about the day you went to the volcano."

"Yes. Did your grandson give you the volcano's replay?"

Barba sighed and seemed to lose himself in thought.

"I went to Thori's funereal this morning," said Stephen. "I thought I might see you there. I had met him last summer."

"Poor soul," Barba lamented. "I was told by those who observed it that his death was an agony. Thori had been ailing for a long time and in his turmoil he turned that poisonous *tsipouro* that aggravated his condition and put bizarre thoughts into his head. In this life man must learn to suffer."

"Some of his thoughts made sense to me."

"You are right; I am not the one to judge his life. We had not been close since Thori left Santorini as a young man to wander. He left his parents to die believing he was dead. Sad, ahmaan. There was a fatal quirk in his nature that prevented him from becoming a human being."

"What was that?"

"It is natural for most men to go through a period of rebellion, though time forces most to forget such notions and rediscover God. Not Thori, his rebellion was too drastic. He never understood that for others to understand and admire a rebellion it had to be minor enough for them to forgive. Thori condemned himself and never belonged in this world. I did pay my final respects to him. This morning before service, I took Kyria Rhea to the church where we could be alone with him."

"Who is she?" Stephen took a long drag off his cigarette.

"She took good care of you eh?" Barba smiled.

"And I never had a chance to thank her."

"No need, she understands life. I would tell you about her but she is too long a story and you would miss your ship," Barba poured Stephen a second glass of wine. "It will have to wait until you return. Consider it a lesson in patience."

They finished their wine and stepped into the saffron colored sunlight together. He offered Barba a cigarette and they walked to the cliff wall.

"As I told you," said Stephen, "I wanted to thank Kyria Rhea before I left but she did not answer my knock."

"Her cat was killed during the storm last night and she has gone to the northern part of the town to adopt his brother. He will be her third Nemean. There is a place there where the strays collect and she knows them all and their lineage."

"Give this to her for me," Stephen took out the money he had coerced from Loutras.

"Just this," Barba selected a hundred drachma bill, the equivalent of a few dollars. "I will see that she gets it. Her needs are few and taken care of."

"But I want her to have it all," Stephen placed the money into Barba's hand and folded his fingers about it. "Give it to her or keep it and use some on her whenever necessary."

"If you insist," the old man put his arm about Stephen and embraced him. "Safe journey. God willing I will be here when you return."

"You have no choice Barba; I hold you to your promise to tell me about Kyria Rhea."

"Remember God Stephanos."

Chapter 57

The horn of the ship *Medea* blasted news of her presence simultaneous to Stephen's arrival at the base of the cliff. There were five animals milling about the trough where he dismounted, indicating that few passengers would be boarding the vessel for Crete.

There was little activity on the dock reminiscent of the hectic scene the night he arrived. Making for the café to retrieve his bags, he saw Nancy and Jill. They sat at a table beneath the awning, drinking bottled water, gazing anxiously in his direction.

All we have is each other, Stephen resigned himself to the situation, and only for a time at that. All reason, all compromises rest on the turn of emotion. They just look good to you today. As he drew close enough to the girls to inhale their perfumes he fantasized about making love to both of them.

"You're late," Jill greeted him with a warm smile. "Will you never gain a concept of time Stephen?"

"I thought I told you not to miss your ship on my account," he said to Nancy.

"Nancy's faith in you was devotional, she was sure you'd make it in time for the second one. So we waited; in case you accidentally missed the first one."

"Are you sorry we did?" asked Nancy.

"I was just imagining what it might be like if the three of us made love," Stephen candidly confessed, curious for Nancy's reaction.

"I like that, if she won't be a sport I'll help you with Nancy," Jill teased her.

"I see you came prepared for the voyage," Nancy changed the direction of the conversation to the wine bottle Stephen carried.

"A gift from the old wine merchant. Remember him?"

"The one who patted our knees while we sampled his wares," said Nancy, "how could I forget him?"

"Since our fate and bodies are now in your hands, would it be rude to inquire where you are leading us?" said Jill.

"To Crete today then maybe to Samos for the wine festival or to Lesbos that's one island you might find particularly interesting."

"Why is that?"

"It's where the ancient poetess Sappho composed her verses and where those rumors about her began and adopted the name of her island to describe them."

"What rumors?" asked Nancy.

"That she was a lesbian," Jill laughed, "you know, from the name of the island. Lesbos, he's having you on. Just how far did you go to entice him? Do you think he believed you?"

"The launch is boarding," said Nancy.

"Reprieved by the boat," Jill laughed again.

The girls lifted their knapsacks from the ground and Stephen his bags from the chair beside him. There were five more passengers on the launch.

"So you are leaving us today," Kapetan Charon said to Stephen after helping the girls to board.

"Yes."

"You chose an auspicious day. This morning a school of dolphins swam past the volcano in the direction of Crete. It would be unfortunate to waste such a good omen."

The crewman cast off the mooring ropes and the boat lurched free from the dock. Soon the girls were using their hands to keep the wind-blown hair from their eyes.

"Definitely more impressive in daylight," said Jill looking back at the cliff and up to Thira. "I imagine if I wanted to die jumping from up there would guarantee the job," she mused. "I wonder for what part of the fall she was conscious?"

"Really Jill, could we leave on a more morbid note?" said Nancy.

"What do you suppose could make someone do such a thing?" said Jill.

"Sappho did it to cure a broken heart, though not from this cliff," said Stephen.

"Genetics," said Nancy with a callousness that made Stephen wonder if she wasn't capable, like their ship's namesake, of destroying her child to punish her husband.

Stephen unzipped his Pan Am bag and removed the manila envelope and reached inside his jacket for his gun. He wanted to tuck it in the bag among his clothes beneath the poetry before boarding the *Medea*. But looking back at Santorini, he felt bitter about the indecisive course of his life.

Do something, he urged himself. A man in chains could not be free and he held his chains in his hands, the poetry in one and the gun in the other. He should rid himself of one, or the other, or both. This was his chance.

His poem should be cast to the wind. After all, it was the experience of creation that was important not the search for affirmation. An artist should destroy his works as he finishes them; but he could not release the envelope.

The gun then. If he did not intend to use it, it should be relegated to the depths of the sea. He held it over the side of the launch, just above the sea that was being broken into a wavy froth by the boat's hull, but could not summon the conviction to release it either.

Perhaps he reasoned that by living beyond his youth he had already committed suicide. Or perhaps he felt that without the gun weakness would deteriorate the fiber of his being until words such as freedom and meaning were supplanted by prayers to the empty sky. That soon he would seek success, no matter how meager, which was an illusion at best, until he was absorbed into the pedestrian stream of nonexistence, finally accepting instead of searching for answers.

"That envelope reminds me, I have something for you," said Jill.

While she rummaged her bag for it, he slipped the gun into his flight bag.

"Here," Jill handed him a sealed white envelope.

"What is it?" he asked.

"I don't know."

"How do you know it's for me?"

"A French girl gave it to her in the taverna last night," said Nancy.

"She took me for your girlfriend," said Jill. "She was with a group catching today's ship to Athens and didn't know how to find you."

Stephen tried to envision that meeting. He took the envelope and booklet of geometric patterns and slipped them into the manila envelope and sealed its clasp and zipped up his flight bag.

"Aren't you going to read it?"

When are journeys over and when have they just begun?

"See how it glistens, Atlantis in the sun," someone said.

Given time,
given space,
oblivion is born.

74955215R00124

Made in the USA
Columbia, SC
09 August 2017